WHAT JANIE FOUND

BOOKS BY CAROLINE B. COONEY

The Lost Songs
Three Black Swans
They Never Came Back
If the Witness Lied
Diamonds in the Shadow
A Friend at Midnight
Hit the Road
Code Orange
The Girl Who Invented Romance
Family Reunion
Goddess of Yesterday
The Ransom of Mercy Carter
Tune In Anytime
Burning Up
What Child Is This?
Driver's Ed
Twenty Pageants Later
Among Friends
The Time Travelers, Volumes I and II

THE JANIE BOOKS
The Face on the Milk Carton
Whatever Happened to Janie?
The Voice on the Radio
What Janie Found
What Janie Saw (an ebook original story)
Janie Face to Face

THE TIME TRAVEL QUARTET
Both Sides of Time
Out of Time
Prisoner of Time
For All Time

BOOKS BY CAROLINE B. COONEY

The Lost Songs
Three Black Swans
They Never Came Back
If the Witness Lied
Diamonds in the Shadow
A Friend at Midnight
Hit the Road
Code Orange
The Girl Who Invented Romance
Family Reunion
Goddess of Yesterday
The Ransom of Mercy Carter
Tune In Anytime
Burning Up
What Child Is This?
Driver's Ed
Twenty Pageants Later
Among Friends
The Time Travelers, Volumes I and II

THE JANIE BOOKS
The Face on the Milk Carton
Whatever Happened to Janie?
The Voice on the Radio
What Janie Found
What Janie Saw (an ebook original story)
Janie Face to Face

THE TIME TRAVEL QUARTET
Both Sides of Time
Out of Time
Prisoner of Time
For All Time

WHAT JANIE FOUND

caroline b. cooney

EMBER

Text copyright © 2000 by Caroline B. Cooney
Cover photographs © 2012 by Anna Subbotina/Shutterstock (silhouette)
and Aleksandr Ugorenkov/Shutterstock (key)

Ember and the E colophon are registered trademarks of Random House, Inc.

Visit us on the Web! randomhouse.com/teens

Educators and librarians, for a variety of teaching tools,
visit us at randomhouse.com/teachers

The Library of Congress has cataloged the hardcover edition of this work as follows:
Cooney, Caroline B.
What Janie found / Caroline B. Cooney. — 1st ed.
p. cm.
Summary: While still adjusting to the reality of having two families, her birth family and the family into which she was kidnapped as a small child, seventeen-year-old Janie makes a shocking discovery about her long-gone kidnapper.
Sequel to: Whatever happened to Janie?
ISBN 978-0-385-32611-7 (hardcover) — ISBN 978-0-375-89208-0 (ebook)
[1. Kidnapping—Fiction. 2. Parent and child—Fiction.
3. Identity—Fiction.] I. Title.
PZ7.C7834 Wg 2000
[Fic]—dc22
99037409

ISBN 978-0-385-74241-2 (tr. pbk.)

RL: 5.3

Printed in the United States of America

10 9 8 7 6 5 4 3 2 1

First Ember Edition 2012

CHAPTER
ONE

Last seen flying west.

Over and over, Janie read those last four words on the report.

I could do that, she thought. I could be "last seen flying west." I too could vanish.

By not being here, I could be a hundred times more powerful and more present. No one could ever set me down. I would control all their lives forever, just by being gone.

She actually considered it.

She didn't worry about the logistics—plane ticket, money, shelter, food, clothing. Janie had never lacked for shampoo or supper or shoes and she couldn't imagine not having them.

She considered this: She could become a bad person.

In the time it took for a jet to cross America, she, Janie Johnson—good daughter, good friend, good student, good sister—with no effort, she could ruin a dozen lives.

She was stunned by the file folder in her fingers, but she was more stunned by how attracted she was to this idea—Janie Johnson, Bad Guy.

In all that had happened—the kidnapping, the new family, the old family, even Reeve's betrayal—nothing had brought such fury to her heart as the contents of this folder.

She couldn't even say, I can't believe it. Because she could believe it easily. It fit in so well. And it made her so terribly angry.

She knew now why her older brother, Stephen, had dreamed for years of college. It was escape, the getaway from his massive store of anger.

She herself had just finished her junior year in high school. If college was the way out, she could not escape until a year from September—unless she escaped the way Hannah had, all those years ago.

Janie Johnson hated her father at that moment with a hatred that was wallpaper on every wall of every room she had ever lived in: stripes and circles and colors of hate pasted over every other emotion.

But gently she slid the police report back into the file folder and put the folder in among the others, pressing with her palm to even up all the folders so that the one that mattered vanished.

It took control to be gentle. Her fingers wanted to crush the contents of the folder, wad everything up and heave it out a window, and then fling the folder to the floor and drag her shoes over it.

The drawer was marked *Paid Bills.* Her father was

MISSING CHILD MILK CARTON CAMPAIGN MARKS ANNIVERSARY

NEW JERSEY (AP)—Today is the anniversary of the "Missing Child Milk Carton" campaign. Launched by Flower Dairy, the campaign placed a photograph of a different missing child every month on the half-pints of milk sold in school cafeterias throughout New Jersey, New York and New England. The campaign was discontinued when some parents felt it was too upsetting for their children.

A spokesperson for Flower Dairy reminded the public, however, of one spectacular success.

Thirteen years earlier, while shopping with her family, three-year-old Jennie Spring had vanished. Mall witnesses saw the child with a young woman, but the woman was not identified. The little girl was never seen again.

The Springs continued to hope they would one day find their daughter. They agreed to put her face on a milk carton. Jennie Spring herself, by then fifteen years old, recognized her photograph.

America was riveted by the story that emerged. The kidnapped child had been raised in a wealthy Connecticut suburb as Janie Johnson. The kidnapping was apparently the act of Hannah Javensen, known to the public because of another drama, in which she joined a cult, and her parents, Frank and Miranda Javensen, stole her back. Javensen had returned to the cult, however, and her parents had never heard from her since.

Why Hannah Javensen kidnapped Jennie Spring is still unknown, but having done so, she evidently panicked and drove across three states to reach the home she had abandoned. She telephoned the parents who had not seen her

(Continued next page)

in years, insisting that the little girl was hers—and therefore their granddaughter. Asking her parents to bring the child up, Hannah Javensen disappeared again.

The Javensens moved, changing their name to Johnson and the little girl's name to Janie to protect their grandchild from the cult and from their daughter.

After the teenage Janie Johnson recognized her face on the milk carton, she was reunited with the Spring family. In the investigation that followed, police and FBI failed to locate Hannah Javensen.

Both the Spring and Johnson families declined comment for this article.

A spokeswoman for Flower Dairy said they remain proud of their part in finding Jennie Spring.

very organized, and now that he could do nothing himself, her mother wanted Janie to be organized in his place. For a few minutes, it had seemed like fun; Janie Johnson, accountant and secretary.

The drawer contained a long row of folders, each with a center label, each label neatly printed in her father's square typewriter-looking print, each in the same blue ink. Folders for water bills and oil bills, insurance policies and tax reports.

And one folder labeled with two initials.

H.J.

It was invisible in the drawer, hidden in the forest of its plain vanilla sisters. But to Janie it flamed and beckoned.

You don't have to stay here, being good and dutiful and kind and thoughtful, said the folder. *You can be Hannah.*

• • •

Reeve Shields was sitting on the floor, his back against the wall, his cutoff jeans and long tan legs sticking out toward Janie. Mrs. Johnson had been sure the project of Mr. Johnson's papers would include plenty of work for Reeve, but so far she had not thought of an assignment for him. That was okay. He was too busy studying Janie to sort papers.

Janie had a very expressive face. Her features were never still but swung from thought to thought. If he could read cheeks and forehead and chin tilt, he could read Janie.

But although he had lived next door to her ever

since he could remember, and although they had once been boyfriend and girlfriend and had been through two hells together, right now he could not read her face.

He did, however, know that he wanted to read the contents of that file. The label was very tempting. The way she had returned it to the drawer, the silence she was keeping—also very tempting.

Don't even think about it, he told himself. How many times are you going to jerk her around? She tells you how to behave, you say, Sure, Janie, and then do exactly what you want. You going to do it now, too? She's speaking to you again, letting you here in the house again, and once again, you can't wait to trespass on her. You promised yourself you'd grow up. So maybe tonight would be a good time. Maybe tonight you should not look in that folder, which obviously contains the most interesting papers Janie has ever seen in her life.

But not for you, sport. Give it up. Offer a distraction, mention dinner, get out of the house, get away from this office, do not interfere.

So Reeve said, "Let's all go get a hamburger. Brian? Janie? Mrs. Johnson? You up for McDonald's? Or you want to go to Beach Burger?"

• • •

"Beach Burger," said Brian Spring quickly. He loved that place. It had its own oceanfront, a tiny little twenty-foot stretch of rock, and you could get your hamburger and fries and milk shake, and leave your socks and shoes in the car, and crawl over the

4

wet slimy rocks and the slippery green seaweed and sit with your toes in the tide. Of course, you had to get back in the car with wet pants and sticky salty skin, but he loved the smell of it: the sea scent you carried home and then, sadly, had to shower off.

Brian felt so included here. It was weird to be part of a large friendly family like his own family in New Jersey and yet never feel included. Up here, visiting Janie (his sister, but not part of his family), he felt strangely more welcome.

That wasn't quite fair.

What he felt was less useless.

He missed his older brother, Stephen, badly. But Stephen was not going to return in any real way. A night here, a week there—but Stephen was gone.

Brian's twin was no company at all, still a shock to Brian, who had thought they would be best friends all their lives. Brendan had not noticed Brian for a whole year. And with the close of school, and the end of baseball (Brendan, of course, was captain and his pitching won the local and regional championships and they even got to the semifinals) and now summer training camps—basketball and soccer—well, the best Brian could do was stand around and help fold his brother's jeans when he packed.

(Brendan even said that. "At least you know how to fold T-shirts," said Bren. "Although I don't screw around with that myself, I just shove 'em in.")

And the other good reason for going to Beach Burger was that Brian wanted food in his hands, so that he wouldn't leap forward and yank that file

5

folder out of Janie's hands. Because he knew in his gut that she had found something important. And everything important to Janie was important to Brian's family. Her other family.

But Brian at this moment did not feel a lot of affection for his own family. No matter what he did there, he was last in line. He was sick of it. Up here in Connecticut with Janie, he wasn't first, but he was part of them, and he wasn't going to wreck that.

What he was going to do, he decided, after the rest of them went to visit Janie's father in the hospital tonight, was walk in here boldly and scope out that folder, as if it were his business.

Because he was pretty sure it was his business.

• • •

Mrs. Johnson was sitting at her own desk, which was at a right angle to her husband's desk, where Janie was studying the bills, paid and unpaid. Mrs. Johnson had been using a small calculator to balance the checking account, and it was making her cry, because this was not her job, had never been her job. In the division of labor that every family requires, checking accounts belonged to her husband.

And now he was in the hospital.

A stroke *and* a heart attack.

She could not believe either of these things.

Frank was slim and strong and he worked out and ate well, and he was still, in her opinion, a young man. Well, not young. But he wasn't old! He was not old enough to have a heart attack. He could

6

not leave her now; he could not die. He could not end up speechless and drooling. She couldn't go through that. She wouldn't go through that.

She had to believe he would recover. Completely.

She mixed up numbers and skipped decimals and could not manage a simple subtraction.

And so she did not see her daughter blazing over the contents of a file folder in Paid Bills, and she did not see Janie's former boyfriend staring in fascination, nor Janie's real brother observing them all.

Mrs. Johnson said, "Yes. Beach Burger. I hope the rocks aren't crowded. I want to sit on the rocks. Don't you, Brian?" She was crazy about Brian. He was such a sweetheart. It was a ridiculous time to have a houseguest, but Brian was a treasure. In a weird way, Miranda Johnson was thrilled and honored to find that her family had extended from here in Connecticut down there into New Jersey, and that somehow, miraculously, she too had been adopted.

It will all work out, she said to herself, and she was actually almost happy. She turned and smiled at the three teenagers, but she did not see how quickly Janie's smile came and went, nor did she attach any importance to Janie's habit of lowering her face to let her heavy dark red hair cover her expression.

● ● ●

Janie got through the whole hamburger thing.

She was pleasant and even funny because she liked the three people with her. But she was aware

7

of her terrible anger sitting next to her on the rock, waiting to come back in, and she could hardly wait to get home, and be by herself, and go back to that folder and let the fury take over.

She thought she could probably produce enough rage to power the house. She could plug the toaster into her hand and burn the bread with her anger.

But no. Once again, she must be controlled and careful and a total fake in front of everybody. Janie Johnson: Good Guy. She was so sick of being good.

"Janie darling," said her mother. Her mother was affectionate with everybody: it was Janie darling and Reeve sweetheart and Brian love.

Did her mother know the truth? It seemed unlikely. Mom would never have let her open that drawer if she had known about the folder in there.

On the other hand, her parents had kept a massive secret for years, and Janie had never suspected a thing. So perhaps they were keeping *two* secrets, and had kept this second secret in front of everybody: the FBI; the police; her Spring family; Reeve; Reeve's lawyer sister, Lizzie; and most of all, Janie herself.

She could not trust either parent now.

"I don't think I'll visit Dad tonight," Janie told her mother, knowing she should tag on some friendly reason, some kindly excuse, like exhaustion. But she was so angry. What if she said, Because I'd rip out the tubes keeping him alive if I had to see him right now?

"I'll drop you guys at home," she said to the boys, "and then drive Mom to the hospital." She checked her watch. Six P.M. Plenty of time to get rid of all three of them, examine that folder, finish screaming and go back to the hospital. "I'll pick you up at nine, Mom."

Janie did all the driving now.

For years, she had dreaded the moment in which she must stop being the passenger and turn into the driver. Had cringed at the thought of facing traffic; flinched at choosing left lane or right.

Janie Johnson had preferred leaning on her parents. But her mother and father had been weakened from finding out that Janie was theirs by theft. They'd so carefully kept a secret all these years—the secret of Janie's birth—but they'd been wrong about what the secret was. They'd never known the real secret.

The media attention and the law, the neighbors and the necessity to face Janie's birth family had quite literally put them both on heart medicine.

Janie had had to become strong for her mother and father, and she'd done it. She was proud of herself. But there had not been quite enough energy to be strong for herself, so she had leaned on Reeve. Probably the most painful mistake she would ever make. Once the possibility of leaning on Reeve was gone, the solution to her problems seemed to be in the driver's seat.

Overnight, Janie wanted a driver's license and a car.

Nothing low to the pavement. No dumb little four-cylinder engine. She wanted height and power. She wanted a cool name. Wrangler or Blazer. (Her best friend, Sarah-Charlotte, suggested a Tracker. "The better to find your kidnapper," said Sarah-Charlotte, as if this were all rather comic. As if anybody at all ever wanted to find the kidnapper.)

The only good thing about the kidnapper was that she had vanished. Nobody in either family had a clue to the kidnapper's whereabouts or even if she was still alive. Finding the kidnapper would destroy all that the Springs and the Johnsons had managed to save.

In the end, Janie chose an Explorer, which her father gladly bought. He was so pleased that Janie wanted to drive, and have power and freedom. It was a big step up for a girl who had spent the winter barely able to turn a page in a magazine.

Now she thought grimly, I don't need a Tracker, do I? And Dad knew that when he bought my Explorer. The kidnapper has already been tracked.

She remembered to be calm. She smiled at her mother, her former boyfriend and her little brother. Then she realized that even when she dropped Mom at the hospital, she would not be alone when she got home.

Brian would be there.

Janie could see no way to unload Brian. No way to shut him up in a guest room while she stormed around screaming.

• • •

It was her careful smile.

Reeve knew it well.

Her real smiles—her laughing, exuberant, I-love-

10

you smiles—he hadn't gotten those since last fall, when he'd been such a massive jerk that he was amazed anybody spoke to him now.

He also knew what she was doing.

If they all went to drop Mrs. Johnson at the hospital, they'd drive home together. Reeve would drift on into the Johnsons' house with Janie and Brian. But Janie didn't want Reeve around, so she'd drop him off first and then go on to the hospital.

It was that folder. She was going back into it when she had no witnesses.

Of course, she'd still have Brian. There was no place to drop Brian.

I could give Janie a present, thought Reeve. I could invite Brian to go to a movie with me. I could say, "Brian, let's give Janie a rest, let's let her have a night on her own." But I'm selfish. I don't want to go to a movie with a fourteen-year-old. I want to go to a movie with Janie and sit in the back and make out. Or at least hold hands.

Not that Janie had allowed any of that since he'd been back from college.

Reeve Shields, he said to himself. Good Guy. "Janie," he said, "you want a rest from us, too? Brian and I could go see a movie."

• • •

Janie's eyes filled. It annoyed her terribly. Was she never going to outgrow these sudden tears?

She knew that he knew something was up.

Reeve studied her all the time, trying to find a way back, trying to find the sentence or the gesture that

11

would make them boyfriend and girlfriend again. "I'd like that," she said. She did not look at Reeve but got up carefully, as if she were worried about falling into the sea. An unexpected swim in salt water would be a pleasure compared to examining that folder at length, and the reason for her care was very different: to show her mother nothing.

I will never show either of my parents anything again, she thought. They had no right to do this. None.

Her mother said, "Janie darling, I know how hard this is on you. Seeing Daddy so collapsed and incapable. It's terrible for all of us. It's so hard to imagine the future. I've asked too much of you, making you go with me and sit by his bedside every night. All three of you must go see a movie. See a fun one. Lots of laughs. You need to laugh, Janie darling."

• • •

In the end, they all drove to the hospital, dropping Mrs. Johnson off with many kisses and assurances of love, and Janie promised a ten-thirty pickup instead of nine, leaving lots of time for the movie they would supposedly see.

Reeve shifted up to the front seat and Brian stayed in back.

Janie was wearing her hair loose. She had serious hair; more, said Sarah-Charlotte, than any three normal people.

Reeve laid claim to a single red curly strand, winding it around his finger. Her hair was long and his finger turned into a shining dark red cylinder.

12

Janie took the curl back without looking at him. Her hair sproinged out past her shoulders and it seemed to Reeve she could not possibly see the traffic; her view had to be blocked by a forest of autumn-red leaves: her own hair.

Janie did not get on the interstate, which was the only road that went to the twelve-screen theater. She drove home. Her house and Reeve's were next door, which was convenient or maddening, however you felt at the moment.

Reeve did not have a car of his own this summer, but his family owned plenty of cars and one was always available; it was just a matter of begging and pleading and then promising to fill the gas tank.

Okay, fine, Reeve said to himself. Janie ignores me; I take her kid brother out instead.

He sighed but, not wanting to hurt Brian's feelings, cut the sigh off. As cheerfully as he could, he said, "So, Bri, what do you want to see?"

And Brian Spring said, "I want to see what was in that folder, Janie."

CHAPTER
TWO

When Stephen Spring went out West for college, he
planned never to go home again. The day he arrived
in Colorado and stood beneath that immense blue
sky and faced that amazing leap of mountains, he
knew he'd done the right thing.

Stephen understood every deserting father from a
Civil War army who, when the war ended, walked
west alone instead of home to his family. He understood every immigrant who ever crossed the sea,
never again to visit the place of his birth.

You could love your family.

Stephen did.

You could love your hometown.

Stephen did.

And you could be so glad that you were gone.
Thousands of miles between you and your history.
Your past was over.

Stephen Spring was glad.

Early on, Stephen stopped using the telephone.

14

If he phoned home, Stephen was so attached to his mother's anxieties that a tremor in her voice cut to the bone. He would close off any conversation too fast, hurting his mother's feelings, saying, "Well, I'm really busy, Mom, I'll call next week."

So now he e-mailed. Voices were too intense. Too much memory living in a voice. Too much pull. E-mail gave the impression of being connected, but nothing of Stephen was taken away.

He hated talking to his twin brothers. Brendan had abandoned Brian, and Stephen knew what pain Brian was in; knew that Brian had let himself get adopted by Janie and her kidnap family. Actual conversation with his little brothers was out. Stephen was furious with Bren for being a lousy twin, and more furious with Brian for becoming a Johnson.

As for his sister Jodie, she was wildly excited by her own freshman year at college, coming up so fast, and he was afraid of her questions; afraid he might actually say to her, You'll love it! You'll never go home again. He missed talking to Jodie. But he couldn't betray his parents with such a conversation.

He knew in a dark place in his heart that his mother and father understood; had understood before he did; had expected nothing else.

Stephen had gone home for Thanksgiving: three days.

For Christmas: four days.

It was almost July and he hadn't been back since. He had to take summer classes, he told his family.

15

Needed the money from his summer job. Might not get home till next Thanksgiving.

Stephen liked the sound of his arguments. He repeated them to himself rather frequently. He was astonished, one day, to walk into a McDonald's and nearly weep at the sight of a family.

They were a boring family, tired and grimy, clothes wrinkled, the mother without makeup, the father in need of a haircut.

The father held the two-year-old, who was whining. The mother held the baby, who had a runny nose. The four-year-old (Stephen, as the oldest of five, knew his toddler ages) was scrounging up french fries that had fallen to the floor and making a ketchup painting on his mound of filthy potatoes.

Stephen got in line to place his order. He had nothing but hamburger thoughts. When the bag of hot burgers and thick milk shake was in his hand, he took another look at the boring family.

Father and son were leaning across the ruined french fries, rubbing noses and laughing. The mother had hoisted the baby into the air over her face, and the baby's giggle filled the room. The two-year-old had stuck his hand down into his father's large soda to pull up ice chips, thrilled in a toddler way as ice melted between his little fingers.

In that moment, Stephen wanted his sister and his brothers and mother and father so fiercely it felt like a heart attack. Tightness in his chest, shortness of breath, clammy hands, genuine fear—classic symptoms of heart failure.

16

In spite of his best efforts, had he left his heart at home?

Stephen barely made it to the truck. It was safer inside the cab with the doors shut against the world. He occupied himself stripping the paper off his straw and squirting ketchup out of its packet.

He gagged on his first bite.

He thought: *sister.* I missed *one* sister.

But I have two of them.

• • •

The bike path crawled up the steep gritty slope of the mountain, curving in long slow S shapes to lessen the grade. Stephen and Kathleen had been gasping for some time, and had finally given up and were walking their bikes.

Stephen was so surprised to find himself with a girlfriend.

His parents would adore Kathleen Marie Donnelly. She was an athlete and a scholar. She was beautiful, courteous and kind. She was Catholic.

In short, she was perfect.

Stephen told her this frequently.

Kathleen had a system in which Stephen earned kisses. Sometimes he could earn thousands of them. At this moment, he had a kiss debt so large he figured it would take years to work it off. Good years.

He had not told his parents about Kathleen.

He never mentioned that he and Kathleen did everything together, especially skiing. Stephen

17

worked overtime to earn money for lift tickets, but his family didn't even know he'd learned how to ski or that most of his friends were more ski bum than student.

When spring semester ended, Kathleen hadn't gone home to California but had stayed on with Stephen, and when they weren't in class or working, they hiked and biked and rented movies. Stephen was as paired with Kathleen as Stephen's twin brothers had once been with one another. How he had envied his little brothers, always possessed of company and a best friend. Now he knew what it was like.

College and Kathleen were softening him.

Without his past to carry around, without explanations and media attention biting his ankles like mean little dogs, Stephen was becoming the person he would have been if the kidnapper had never driven into their lives.

His childhood had exhausted him. The pressure of staying safe, of not being the next one kidnapped, never letting his parents down, keeping his brothers and sister in sight—it was all the family time he could bear.

He was done with families.

Stephen knew girls well. In their tiny house in New Jersey, Jodie's girlfriends were over all the time. Relentlessly they talked, and he could never get away from the steady drone of syllables and the trill of giggles. Stephen knew that girls moved into the future faster than a boy could shift gears in a truck.

Put one kiss on a girl's lips, and she'd be drafting wedding invitations.

One more kiss, and she'd be choosing names for their children. Designing the living room in their first house.

Stephen figured if he never told Kathleen about his family, he'd be safe. He didn't want a family of his own.

The bike path became even steeper. To his right, the mountain fell away in a rocky scree that looked as if it had recently suffered a rock slide. Sweat ran down Stephen's body. He loved sweat.

He had a great sweaty job this summer. More than anything—more than Kathleen—he loved his job.

In New Jersey, if you wanted green grass, you just stood there. It grew; you mowed. But in Colorado, green was not a normal color. If you stood there and looked at your front yard, it would be parched and dusty. Around here, grass required an underground sprinkler system.

Stephen had gotten a job installing sprinklers. He loved the sun overhead and the bandanna he tied over his forehead to keep sweat out of his eyes. He loved his bare chest, and the deep tan he acquired, and the physical strength.

His locked-up childhood had given him inner strength, which was fine, and he understood why people the world over were hunting for inner strength, while Stephen had enough to go around twice—but it was outer strength Stephen craved. True muscle.

19

He had it.

Riding his bike, Stephen had thought only about the path beneath his tires. But on foot, he was taken by the loose rocks everywhere. Rocks demanded kicking. He kicked a pebble the size of a golf ball, and it ricocheted down the mountainside, pinging off other rocks.

He kicked a rock the size of a soccer ball. He didn't expect it to move. He figured he'd dent his toes. But it was precariously balanced on gravel and tumbled instantly and loudly down the hill, and Stephen's body, off center from the kick, began to follow.

His bike went first, and in that split second when he could have chosen to let go of the bike, he didn't. He felt the skid of gravel under his sneakers, the greed of gravity stretching out for him; claiming him.

Gravity wanted everything, and wanted it fast, and wanted Stephen.

He had time to think: *I never got my revenge.*

And then he was out of time, and there was nothing but the fall itself.

Kathleen hurled her bike aside, leaped forward and grabbed at him. She missed, tried again and got the sleeve of his T-shirt. Now they both fell, scraping along the scree, hands and shoes flailing for a ledge. Ten feet down they found a grip.

"You jerk," said Kathleen.

His T-shirt sleeve had ripped off. It slid down his arm and hung around his wrist, a limp white cotton bracelet.

They crawled back to the path, trembling, knee-caps and elbows bleeding. "Staying alive is the first step, Stephen," said Kathleen.

He glanced down where they had fallen and had a strange vivid picture of himself pushing the kidnapper off this very ledge. How good it would feel to watch while the kidnapper screamed and broke and snapped. Stephen would kick stones after her—big ones; sharp ones—and they would crush her and—

He stopped himself. He accepted a swig from Kathleen's water bottle. You're a civilized person, he told himself. You don't dream of hurling people off cliffs and clapping as they die.

• • •

Farther up was a level place where they could assess the damage to Stephen's bike.

Stephen yanked the bill of his cap down, as if shading his eyes from the bright sun, but he was just hiding. Sometimes he felt like a car, choking on the exhaust of his childhood.

Five happy children in the Spring family.

And then there were four.

Skip the things that could have happened to the missing child.

What about the four who were left?

Stephen had been the jailer for Jodie and Brendan and Brian: the escort, the giver of permission, the fender-off of kidnappers. The oldest had to keep the others safe. The oldest did the head counts and checked the locks.

When they had found his baby sister, Jennie, and

found that Jennie had become Janie; that the man and woman Janie lovingly called Daddy and Mommy were in fact the *parents* of the kidnapper, Stephen expected hideous things to happen to Frank and Miranda Johnson.

But nothing had happened to the Johnsons!

Having failed with their real daughter, Frank and Miranda got to keep their stolen kid. They were allowed to go on pretending that Jennie was their own. They even got to call her by the name they'd chosen, Janie, instead of her real name, Jennie. *They* were the ones who got a second chance. Not Stephen's parents.

Maddeningly, everybody believed the Johnsons. ("Oh, we didn't realize," insisted Mr. and Mrs. Johnson. "We thought she was Hannah's little girl. We thought she was our granddaughter. We changed our names and disappeared and pretended to be Janie's parents because the cult would come and get our little girl.")

Right.

Like that could possibly be the truth.

Yet the FBI, the New Jersey state police and the local police let this flimsy story pass. Even Stephen's mother and father accepted this ludicrous version of why their little girl grew up as Janie Johnson. She's happy, she's safe, said Stephen's parents, and we must rejoice to have her back at all.

Stephen hadn't seen anything to rejoice about.

But revenge was out of fashion. You were supposed to feel people's pain. Sympathize with their unfortunate choices. Make allowance for any vice they might accidentally have acquired.

Stephen was the only one who believed there had to be a prison somewhere that was just right for Frank and Miranda Johnson.

He slid a thin slab of rock between the bent frame and the front wheel and used it as a lever to force the frame back into shape. He shoved so hard it bent in the other direction.

"Calm down," said Kathleen. "You have enough adrenaline in you, you could probably reshape the bike with your teeth."

Stephen pretended to laugh.

"I finally heard from my parents, by the way," said Kathleen. "They're coming next weekend. I can't wait for them to meet you." She tipped up the bill of his cap and kissed his eyelids. "They'll love you, Stephen. We're going to have dinner at the Boulderado. I want you to wear your khaki pants, I'm going to iron them, and your yellow shirt, I'll iron that, too."

But Stephen dreaded the thought of another family. He had refused to become friends with Janie's Connecticut family and he did not feel up to impressing Kathleen's California family. One family in this world was plenty.

CHAPTER
THREE

"What folder?" said Janie to her little brother. She tried to keep her voice breezy, but instead it broke.

She turned into her driveway. Small green bushes divided hers from Reeve's. She suppressed the urge to drive over them and flatten them, just to be stronger than something. She parked by the side door. The Johnsons didn't use their garage. It was full of stuff. Cars hadn't fit for years.

She took the keys out of the ignition and put her hands up to protect her face. The instant she no longer had the task of driving, tears attacked.

The boys sat waiting for her to get control back. They weren't going to open their car doors till she did and she didn't want to leave the safe tidy enclosure of a vehicle.

"You give everything away, Janie," explained her brother. "Your face shows everything you're thinking."

At that moment, Janie could have given them all

away: every person related to her, and every person who pretended to be.

Pretending was fine when you were little and pretended with dolls or blocks or wooden trains. But to pretend forever? To find, once more, that her life was a fantasy spun by the people who supposedly loved her?

She stared at her home, a big old shingled house modernized with great slabs and chunks of window. So many lies hidden behind such clear glass. Her unshed tears were so hot she thought they might burn her eyes and leave her blind.

I stayed here! she thought. I gave up my birth family to come back here.

The irony of it burned as badly as tears.

"The label on the file folder," said Reeve very softly, "was H. J."

Janie flattened her hands on her cheeks and pressed inward toward her nose, squashing everything against its freckled tip. "H. J.," she said, voice squeezed between her lips like toothpaste, "stands for Hunting Jaguars."

They all knew what H. J. stood for. But Reeve let it go. "Hex on Jellybeans," he agreed.

I could hex a few people right now, she thought. I'm not ready for this! I've never been ready. I wasn't ready to find out my parents aren't my parents. I wasn't ready to find out I was kidnapped. I wasn't ready to have Reeve sell me on his radio show. I wasn't ready to have my Connecticut father suffer a heart attack and a stroke. And I'm not ready to find out that he—

"Perfect timing!" called a sharp high voice, and sharp high heels stabbed steps and pavement.

Of Reeve's two older sisters and one older brother, Lizzie was the scary one. Thinner than anybody, not tall, not beautiful, she didn't walk, she stalked. Her frown started upward from her chin instead of downward from her forehead, and you fell into her frown, ready to confess to anything.

As a courtroom lawyer she must be terrifying. Janie could imagine juries cowering in their corner; witnesses desperate to please. How relieved everybody in Connecticut had been when Lizzie decided to practice law in California.

And now Lizzie was in love.

This was amazing, but more amazing was that some man had fallen in love with Lizzie. Who would want to spend a lifetime in the same apartment as Lizzie Shields? Everybody was eager to meet William.

"Come inside, Janie," said Lizzie sternly. "We'll measure you."

Can't make it, Lizzie, thought Janie. I have a temper tantrum waiting. A file folder to study. Police reports. I probably need to assassinate somebody.

But this was a chance to dump Reeve and Brian. When Janie went back into that folder, it must be without people who could read her thoughts.

She opened her door before Lizzie could get closer. I'm never letting anybody get closer again, she thought. Distance is the thing. I can keep Lizzie at a distance. Wedding talk will do it. "What did you decide, Lizzie?" she asked, in a voice as fluffy as a summer gown. "Long? Short? Flowered? Satin?"

"Huh?" said Brian.

"This is about dresses," Reeve explained. "Lizzie's getting married. She's home to make wedding plans. I'm an usher, Janie's a bridesmaid. Come on, Brian, we'll file folder later."

Janie shot him a look. He made a time-out signal with his hands and said quickly, "We'll ask Janie if she'll let us file folder later when she file folders."

Before, when Reeve signaled capital *T*, it meant: Time to be alone together. Now it meant: Don't yell at me. I'm stupid, but I'm nice.

Janie followed Lizzie into the Shields house. Reeve and Brian trailed. "When is the wedding?" asked Brian.

"July twentieth," said Lizzie, as if nothing else could ever happen on that date. It was hers. She owned it.

Mrs. Shields flung open the door. Reeve's mother might be fifty-five and chubby, but she was hopping up and down like a little girl with a jump rope. She was a happy woman. She had never expected Lizzie to have a traditional wedding. Or any wedding.

"Hello, everybody!" caroled Mrs. Shields. "How's your mother holding up, Janie?" She didn't wait for an answer. "You will love the fabric Lizzie chose! It'll look so nice against your red hair."

Janie could not picture Lizzie choosing fab-

27

ric. Choosing candidates for sheriff, maybe, but cloth?

Out came measuring tape and a little notebook covered in white satin and lace.

"Tell me you didn't buy that yourself," Janie said. Lizzie's accessories generally had sharp edges.

Lizzie turned a little pink. "I had to write the details down in something, didn't I?"

"Wow," said Janie.

"Throws you off, doesn't it?" agreed Reeve. He shot Janie the twinkle-eyed grin she used to adore. *I still adore the grin,* she thought, *I'm just not sure of the person behind it.*

Reeve poked Lizzie. "Just when you think you know your tough old sister, she turns out to be this sentimental, waltzing—"

"Reeve, don't start anything," said his mother.

"Lizzie started it," said Reeve.

"William, actually," said Lizzie, looking soft and pretty.

Janie had a sudden wave of nausea and had to cross the room, pretending interest in stacks of brides' magazines with Post-its marking their pages. *Don't start anything. If I go back to that folder, I'm sure starting something. Or finishing it.*

But if I don't go back to that folder, the facts are still in it.

If only I hadn't agreed to handle the bills while Daddy's sick.

If only.

My whole life comes down to that: If only.

"Lizzie darling, while you have your notebook open," said Mrs. Shields, "let's schedule the bridesmaids' luncheon."

"Cut," said Lizzie. "I'd be bored."

That was the Lizzie they knew and occasionally liked—as long as she didn't stay too long.

"Well, at least choose the restaurant for the after-rehearsal dinner," said her mother.

"No rehearsal. We're grown-ups. We know how to walk down an aisle."

Even Janie had to laugh. Lizzie was edging up toward romance, but she couldn't quite touch it. How astonishing that Lizzie could be more romantic than Janie. "At least we'll have great dresses, right?" she said to Lizzie. "Let me see the picture of my dress. What am I wearing?"

Lizzie opened her notebook to the page where she'd taped magazine cutouts of the gowns she had chosen. Reeve and Brian crowded in to see too. Reeve put his hand on Janie's shoulder.

"It's beautiful!" cried Janie. Partly to extricate herself from Reeve's touch, she forced Lizzie into a swoon, and the two of them fell backward onto the sofa. "That," said Janie, "is the most romantic, the laciest and the most backless dress in the whole world. Now show me your gown, it must be even more beautiful."

Lizzie turned the page.

Janie sat up straight. "Oh, Lizzie," she breathed. "William is going to pass out at the sight of you. You are going to be the loveliest bride on earth."

29

Brian felt as he so often did around girls. They were another species. He should be taking notes. Field observations.

How disappointing that the file folder was just about H. J.

Brian had hoped for something really bad and exciting. It wasn't. Naturally Mr. Johnson would keep a file on his long-lost daughter. Paid Bills had seemed like the wrong drawer, but as they drove from beach to hospital to here, Brian had figured out that Mr. Johnson would have paid for a private detective and attorneys and stuff, back when he was trying to get Hannah out of the cult. His daughter was a Paid Bill, just like everybody else's daughter, except that everybody else was writing out checks for braces or college.

Brian wondered vaguely why Lizzie would have asked Janie to be in her wedding. Weren't bridesmaids your girlfriends from slumber parties, like his sister Jodie's endless overnight crowd? But Janie was just a girl next door—and at least ten years younger. In fact, Lizzie had baby-sat for Janie. How come Lizzie didn't have just law school friends in her wedding?

Across the room, as clear as handwriting, a look passed between Reeve and Lizzie.

Reeve *asked* Lizzie to ask Janie! thought Brian. I bet he wants to be in all kinds of romantic gooey situations with my sister, and what's romanticker and gooier than a wedding?

Reeve had let them all down, and Janie was doing the right thing to keep him at a distance. But on July twentieth, Reeve would be handsome and perfect in one of those black wedding outfits with the starched collar and the ascot, and Janie would look like a British princess in that poofy dress, and she and Reeve would probably even walk down the aisle together. Dance at the reception together.

And get back together.

And that would be wrong.

Brian could not help liking Reeve.

But Reeve had hurt them all. He didn't deserve Janie back.

• • •

Janie was touched to be a bridesmaid. That Lizzie should even need bridesmaids was touching. Everybody had expected Lizzie to find a justice of the peace and wrap up her marriage ceremony in three minutes or less.

It was Lizzie to whom Janie had turned when she recognized her face on the milk carton. Without Lizzie, Janie might have been frozen in place for years. It was an honor to be her bridesmaid.

Honor.

A wedding word. A Ten Commandments word.

I'm sick of honoring my father and mother, thought Janie. They didn't honor me.

Unbidden, her other father and mother sprang to her mind.

Had she honored her New Jersey parents?

But that was a failure to shove away, and Janie

turned physically from the thought, keeping her back to New Jersey, and instead she considered the police report on Hannah Javensen.

Last seen flying west.

What an evocative word *west* was. Laden with distance and departure.

Did every son and daughter have a moment in which the only possible reaction was: I'm going?

I'm *never* coming back. You'll *never* see me again. I'm out of here, I'm heading west.

But you got over it in an hour. Or a year.

Whoever really just left? Never dialed a phone, never came home for Thanksgiving? That was the thing Janie had always gotten stuck on. The neverness of it. It was like a bad argument in a bad textbook. Between a parent and a child, was there ever really a never?

And how right she had been to suspect that theory.

Of course Hannah had been in touch.

When the phone shrilled, Janie jumped guiltily, as if she were doing something forbidden.

But I am, she thought. I have touched the past.

Mrs. Shields answered the phone and she turned pale and shocked. She looked sadly at Janie. "Oh, Miranda," she said into the phone. "I'm so sorry. Yes, Janie is right here."

He's dead, thought Janie. My father is dead. All the technology and all the doctors failed.

But instead of grief, she just felt more anger.

How dare he die now? How dare he leave her with that folder? Now it was too late for explanations.

With him dead, she could not confront, and scream, and tell him how much she hated him.

Or how much she loved him.

She felt like a tiny child strapped into a huge swing; no way to put her feet on the ground, scuff herself to a halt and jump off.

She took the phone. What do I say to my mother? What comfort do I offer?

Images of her father wavered in her mind, like heat devils on asphalt.

He loved good food and good company. He loved coaching after-school sports, always willing to take on a team nobody else wanted, like ninth grade or junior varsity. He loved watching TV with Janie and couldn't stand it if she left the room and he had to watch alone. He loved documentaries, which Janie despised, but if she flounced out, he'd increase the volume until the house shook with World War II battles or life on coral reefs. He wouldn't lower the volume until she surrendered. He liked neatness, the edges of things lined up, a tablecloth hanging the same number of inches all the way around. He liked laughing.

He liked secrets, thought Janie, and she had been right about the tears; they did burn; her cheeks were scorched where they fell.

Oh, Daddy! she thought. Please don't be dead. I love you. Stay with us.

Her mother's voice was thready and frayed. "They put him back in Intensive Care, Janie. I need you. Please come."

He wasn't dead after all. He was just closer to it.

She got clammy, growing so cold she seemed to be shutting down; her machinery freezing up and failing. "I'll be there in twenty minutes, Mom," she said. And forced from her lips the dutiful sentence, "I love you."

She did not love anybody right now.

She hung up. Her body felt clumsy and unoccupied.

"I'll drive you, Janie," said Reeve, eager to be involved. "I'll stay at the hospital with you. Run errands."

"No, thank you, Reeve." She felt carved from ice. The warm breath of another person might melt her. "But may Brian spend the night here with you guys? Then I don't have to worry about Brian or what time Mom and I get home."

• • •

Brian did not want to stay with the neighbors. He wanted to be useful. Or at least not in the way. But it got settled without him, Mrs. Shields discussing available beds and Janie sweeping him across the two driveways into her house to get his pajamas and toothbrush.

"Janie," he protested, "let me stay here. I'm fine by myself. I'm not a little kid. I can answer the phone and stuff."

She shook her head. "There's an answering machine. Got everything?"

Brian nodded, defeated. She ushered him out into

the warm night and locked the door after them. He knew why she wanted him at Reeve's. She did not trust him. Alone in her house, so near the desk with the folder, he might be tempted to tiptoe into that office. Open that long drawer. Find out what paper had burned her fingers.

"I hope your father is okay," he said. Except that Janie's father was not the man in the hospital bed. Brian's father was Janie's father. "Drive carefully," he said, feeling stupid. Of course she would drive carefully; Janie was an extremely careful kind of person.

Reeve was standing in the drive, backlit by the lights from his house, frontlit by the lights from Janie's. Even to Brian he looked puppy-eager and puppy-sweet. "Janie, are you all right?" he said anxiously.

She got into the Explorer, not swayed by pleading eyes. "It'll be easier once I get to the hospital and see."

"I'll go with you," he offered a second time.

"No, thanks."

Reeve seemed to tremble on the edge of a move.

Don't mention the folder, thought Brian. That would be a mistake. It isn't as important as her father. You bring up the folder, she'll think less of you.

He remembered that he *wanted* Janie to think less of Reeve.

But he thought that in some way, Janie needed Reeve not to be a jerk. So Brian would have to be the

jerk faster. "Are you going to look at the folder without us?" he asked her.

That worked. She gave him exactly the look a jerk
deserved, started the engine and put her Explorer in
reverse. Through the open window, she said, "No.
I'm going to burn it."

CHAPTER
FOUR

Would she burn the folder?

It was appealing. The strike of a match. The burst of flame.

Shredding was trendier but would be more mechanical, and surely not so satisfying.

Janie and her mother were allowed five minutes in Intensive Care. She could think of no way to refuse, so she followed the nurse and her mother through glass doors into a room with four patients and an overdose of clicking, beeping, humming monitors.

Lying on the bed before them was a man punctured with tubes, sunken and pale and in need of a shave. She would not have known who this was. She would have said, Oh, the poor man, his poor family, and then walked on, looking for her father.

Janie's mother took her husband's hand, over and over telling Frank how much she loved him. He looked like pie dough, rolled out flat and thin.

You knew, thought Janie, staring at him. You always knew. When the FBI came, when the police came, when my real parents came—you knew, *and you never told*. Nobody ever read *your* face, Frank Johnson.

Her fingers felt like pencils that she could snap in half and throw away.

This is my father, she said to herself. I love him, and if he dies, it would be terrible.

But the thought sprang up: *So there, Frank Johnson. This is your punishment.*

• • •

They were serious about the five-minute rule. Miranda Johnson knew that, but each time, it upset her to be sent out.

The waiting room was carpeted in blue and wallpapered in flowers. A television was softly delivering the news, as if, in this dreadful place, any news mattered except news of your own family.

Miranda Johnson thought of the daughter she and Frank had been so happy to have, so many years ago. Hannah. A fragile child, desperately shy. Never a best friend. Always on the fringes.

How could a parent solve that? You couldn't buy friends; you couldn't teach friends.

And then the thing they dreamed of ("At college, she'll find friends") happened. Hannah did find a group. A cult, whose leader told Hannah that her parents had no value. Hannah must discard them.

Parents do not matter, said the cult. They will not matter again.

How vividly Miranda remembered the college visit when she and Frank first understood; shaking her daughter's shoulder, shrieking, "These people are sick! They will ruin you!"

But Hannah's friends had told her to expect this. Her parents would try to wreck her new life.

So Hannah vanished, going west to the cult's headquarters, never answering the letters her parents wrote over the years. Never agreeing to a compromise. Not one childhood hug or good-night kiss or gently applied Band-Aid mattered. Hannah shrugged off her first eighteen years as if they had never been.

How joyful then, that sunny afternoon more than a dozen years ago when Hannah had appeared on the doorstep with an adorable daughter of her own. Still thin and pale, eyes still full of confusion, shining hair an eerie halo, Hannah had been clear about one thing: *You raise my child.*

And Miranda and Frank were clear about one thing: *They would.*

And that meant flight.

The cult, whose leaders they knew all too well, whose attorneys and thugs they had met in the years of trying to get Hannah out, would regard this beautiful little girl as their property.

We look young enough to have a toddler, Frank and Miranda said to each other. We'll say we're the mommy and daddy. Who's to know?

And their last name—Javensen; so unusual; so memorable—drop it. From now on, their name would be Johnson.

Their disappearance was accomplished with such speed and efficiency that afterward Miranda could never quite believe she was the one who had pulled it off. There must have been a team.

But no. It was just Frank and Miranda.

Goal: raise Janie as their own.

Aced.

Goal: never tell anybody, lest their address filter back to the cult.

Aced.

Goal: this time around, raise a daughter who would not fall for lies.

Aced.

Because Janie had discovered the worst lie of all. And she had done exactly what Frank and Miranda had raised her to do: uncovered the lie, kicked it around and forced everyone to face it.

There was only one problem.

It was not the lie Frank and Miranda had thought it was.

For this was not Hannah's daughter. This was a stranger's baby Hannah had coaxed out of a mall and into her car. Hannah was a plain old vicious criminal. The worst kind. Not a thief of property or money, of cars or coins.

She had stolen a child.

There were actually very few kidnappings. Two hundred fifty million people in America, and in any given year, hardly fifty children taken by strangers. More people were struck by lightning.

Every time she remembered that her very own

daughter, the child of her body and heart, had committed such an evil, Miranda Johnson was struck by lightning too.

Frank is dying, she thought, staring at the flowered wallpaper of the waiting room. If I had a way to reach Hannah, would I ask her to come? Would she bother to come? Would she say, *I loved you all along?* Would she say, *I'm sorry?*

Would she care what our lives have been—and what they have not?

Hannah, she thought, if Frank dies, you killed him.

• • •

Brian was grumpy. He yanked so hard on the covers of his borrowed bed that the sheets came undone and the whole thing fell on the floor in a slump of blue-and-white stripes. Who needed sheets anyway? Bare mattresses suited Brian's mood. "Janie's making me stay at your house so I'm not at her house sneaking a look at that folder," he said irritably to Reeve.

Reeve nodded. "I picked up on that."

"I bet your mother has a key to their house, Reeve. You guys are that kind of next-door neighbors."

Reeve gave him a long look. "Listen, Brian. Last winter, I dropped from boyfriend to scum in one semester. I believe the issue was trust. As in, nobody trusted me. Remember that? Remember they were right? Remember you were one of the people who wanted to chain me in a car and give me my own stick of dynamite to hold?"

Brian remembered.

"Janie is showing signs of considering me mildly acceptable again. So your plan is that I break into her house, read the folder she's ordered us not to open and then come back and tell you everything. I bet breakfast you'd tell on me, and I'd be back at the trust issue and the scum level."

"That was my plan," agreed Brian.

They both laughed.

What he had done hit Reeve sometimes, when he wasn't busy enough or the house was too quiet. He would get a sick feeling in his chest. Dented, as if he'd been hit by a car.

He knew that Janie had forgiven him in a technical sense; it had happened, it was over. But she had not forgiven him in a real sense. They were just neighbors now.

"Janie wanted to rip that folder into pieces," Brian said. "But it's reasonable for her father to keep a file on Hannah. She was his kid. So what could have been in there to get Janie so upset?"

Reeve began making Brian's bed again. It was something to do.

"Do you think she'll burn it before we get to look at it?" asked Brian.

Reeve yanked the bottom sheet taut. "I just hope she doesn't burn it before *she* gets to look at it. If there are answers, shouldn't she read them?"

They tucked the top sheet in.

Reeve felt a tremor run down his back.

Answers to what? There are no more questions, he thought. We know what happened.

Or do we?

• • •

I won't burn it, Janie decided. I need to read every page carefully. I need to find out what that small packet in the bottom of the folder is.

She knew what the packet was. The size and thickness were distinctive. It was a checkbook. There was a reason H. J. had been filed under Paid Bills.

How long? she thought. What day, what year, did it begin?

Was I three? Six? Eleven?

Taking flute lessons? Horseback riding?

Was it the year we went to Bermuda? The year we took a cruise to Mexico?

All that time, did he know?

"What are you thinking about?" asked her mother.

Janie reminded herself to show nothing. "The paperwork we still have to go through."

Can I bury his secret with him? she thought. Throw that file folder into the coffin and seal them both forever?

"I don't even know what he earns," said her mother gloomily.

"Mother! Are you serious? Of course you know what Dad earns."

"I don't, though. It's ridiculous in this day and age. I realize women have to know their financial circumstances, but I've always said to myself, Well,

43

except if they're married to Frank. Frank takes care of every detail."

Yes, thought Janie, he certainly does. "Does Dad give you an allowance?"

"No, I have that income from my mother's estate. Frank pays for the big things, and anything else, I get. It works fine. We've never quarreled about money like other couples."

Janie's other family had had terrible fights about money.

After the kidnapping, the Springs had stayed in the tiny cramped house long after they could afford a bigger one. There was always at least one person yelling, "She's dead! Whoever kidnapped Jennie killed her! There's no point in staying here! She was little! She didn't know her address or phone number *then,* she's not going to know it *now*! Can we please move to a decent house where we have some space?"

Stephen, Jodie, Brendan and Brian always wanted the best brand of sneakers and the widest television screen, while Mr. and Mrs. Spring were thrifty and wanted to find sneakers on sale and repair the old TV.

But Janie (with her kidnap family, though she hadn't known) rarely gave money a thought. When she asked for something, it was given to her.

Hannah, the kidnapper, had asked for something, and Frank, the father, had given it to her.

And Janie? The somewhat sister? The pretend daughter? Did she go on giving? Or did she take away?

CHAPTER
FIVE

Reeve flicked the chain saw on.

He was the new guy at a tree company, pruning branches and clearing the scrub that had grown up under a power line. Reeve loved the noise and kick of his chain saw. He loved the paycheck. What he didn't love was having no car.

His punishment for poor grades at college was to pay his own car insurance and he hadn't come up with it. Every morning at six A.M., he had to jog to the corner where the crew picked him up.

He liked getting up early, though, standing at the kitchen window to eat his cornflakes, looking out over Janie's backyard.

His latest peace offering was tickets to come see him race. Well, he didn't actually race, he wasn't the driver. He was pit crew. Here too he was the new guy who knew nothing. Reeve was lucky, though, he never minded knowing nothing. He didn't get embarrassed. He just said, "Show me once and then I'll know." That usually worked. If it didn't, he said, "Show me again," and that did work.

He was so happy that Janie had agreed to come.

Mr. Johnson had improved slightly, and Mrs. Johnson was able to smile a little, and Janie felt free to be out of reach for a day.

The topic of file folders had not come up again.

Reeve ran branches through the wood chipper and puzzled over Janie's reaction to that folder. But he got nowhere, and his thoughts turned to cars and engines, a short oval track and Janie laughing.

His failures and stupidity were clearing away like a bad storm going out to sea. The sky was bright, he wasn't so crummy after all, and he had his own chain saw.

• • •

Janie had never been to a car race. Occasionally, flicking the remote, she passed through car races on sports channels while she searched for interesting television. Who would go sit on bleachers just to watch cars travel in circles? It wasn't a sport, it was traffic.

She wanted Sarah-Charlotte's burbly chatter at the races. Nobody was as reliable for being silly as Sarah-Charlotte. How nice it would be to giggle and act twelve, instead of watching death draw close and pull away, like tides rising and falling around her father. All week she had tried to love Dad again and forget the papers in the folder. But the tug of going west got stronger and deeper.

"Hi, Mrs. Sherwood," said Janie into the phone. "May I speak to Sarah-Charlotte?"

Besides, with Sarah-Charlotte along, a day at the races would not be a date with Reeve.

"Janie," said Mrs. Sherwood in her comfort voice. "How's your father doing? We're so worried."

"He's a little better, thanks. We had a scare the other day, but he's back out of Intensive Care and the doctors are more hopeful."

"Your family has suffered so much," said Mrs. Sherwood. "It's unfair that any of you should suffer again."

As if there were a referee on the sidelines to keep life fair, calling foul during kidnaps or issuing penalities for family-destroying lies.

If I go back into that folder, Janie thought, I'll be hostage again, kidnapped again, a three-year-old again. But if I don't, I'll never know what's really there.

She swallowed. "Reeve gave me tickets for the car race on Saturday," she said brightly. "I was hoping Sarah-Charlotte could drive up with me for the day."

Hoping? Needing.

Mrs. Sherwood laughed out loud at the idea of Sarah-Charlotte having time. "Sarah-Charlotte's at work, Janie. Last week she had three articles in the paper. We've started a scrapbook."

During the school year, Sarah-Charlotte had started covering school sports for the local weekly. This summer she was so busy rushing from field to pool to court, Janie had not seen her since the last day of school.

How young Janie felt. Sarah-Charlotte had become a woman with a career, while Janie was just a kid living in the past. "Thanks anyway," she said lamely. She tried not to think of the summer job at the stable she'd had to quit because she was needed at home.

She phoned Adair next.

"I don't know when she'll be home," said Adair's brother. "She lifeguards every day, you know, and waitresses at night."

Janie did not usually have to beg for a girlfriend. "Is she working Saturday?"

"Sure. Always."

Only a few weeks ago, the girls had been phoning back and forth constantly. She'd known every hour of their schedules. Now she knew nothing.

I like knowing, she thought. I like knowing phone numbers and plans and what everybody's wearing. I want all my knowing settled around me like blankets on a bed. And here I am again, and I know nothing and I never have.

She tried Katrina, who was a day camp counselor and despised it. "I'm never having children of my own," Katrina had told Janie after the first week of camp. "It turns out I'm a monster, and I like only polite clean people, and there's no such thing if you're eight."

"Hi there!" cried Katrina's answering machine. "Nobody can—"

Janie hung up, speaking quickly before the sense

48

of exclusion could drown her. "Well, Brian," Janie said to her brother, who was hovering on the far side of the room, "it's you and me."

His twin was robust and brawny, but Brian was still thin; thin bones, thin chest. Still a child. "Are you sure you want me?" he said uncertainly.

This is how Hannah fell into the cult, Janie thought. Nobody wanted her. Like me today, or Brian tomorrow.

She flung her arms around her brother. "You're the best thing in my summer. Of course I want you. I was just calling people so we'd have a crowd. But you and I can party by ourselves."

"Without Reeve?"

"He'll be in the pits. We'll be in the stands."

• • •

Saturday was toasty and gold, a light wind lifting clouds in a sky of blue. Janie drove while Brian stared out the window. He felt ageless, as if being fourteen meant nothing; he was as old as the world and as young as the day. He was happy.

Reeve was waiting for them at the ticket window, where he got Janie a pit pass. It was a bracelet made of heavy paper in an orange-and-black checkered flag pattern. "I'm pit crew?" said Janie happily. "I don't even know how to change a tire."

"It's just identification so you can hang out with me some of the time," said Reeve. "Brian, I'm sorry, but you're under sixteen and you can't be in the pits. You have to stay on the bleachers."

"It's okay. I brought a book," said Brian, who always brought a book. He had gotten hooked on the Trojan War. After he read *The Iliad*—a wonderfully violent book; did any other author dwell so affectionately on stabbing people's eyes out?—he began collecting pictures of the Trojan horse. He photocopied everything in the library and downloaded everything he could find on the Net.

He was fascinated by the idea of giving a present to the enemy. A present so magnificent they forgot you were the bad guy.

But now he was just hungry. It was hollow screaming hunger, as if ten hamburgers couldn't fill him up. Maybe, thought Brian hopefully, I'm about to grow. This is pre-tallness hunger.

He pictured himself six feet tall like Reeve or Stephen. Passing Brendan.

The back of somebody's pickup truck was filled with coolers and bags of food and six-packs of soda for the driver, crew, girlfriends and boyfriends.

"I packed a separate cooler for you," Reeve said to Brian, "so you won't run out of food and be lost up there without us."

Rats, thought Brian. I knew this would happen. I'll like Reeve again.

• • •

Brian and Janie tried numerous bleacher locations.

High. Low. Facing the sun. Backs to the sun.

They settled on the topmost row, the only seats where you could lean back and get comfortable. The races were immensely more fun than either of them had expected. Brian had not opened his book.

They had no money with them to place bets so they divided their sandwiches into quarters and bet with food. Brian had lost his entire sandwich, and Janie was keeping it.

"Some sister," said Brian.

"It was a bet," said Janie. "You lost."

"I'll starve to death."

"Oh, well."

"Please can I have half my sandwich?"

"Pick a winning car, it's your only hope."

The dirt track was cracked and dry, beaten down by tires that scoured its surface. Dust filled their eyes. Reeve had instructed Janie to wear crummy old clothes and she was grateful. She and her outfit were turning gray. Grit sifted into her hair and settled on the back of her neck.

Crowds yelled, loudspeakers shrieked, engines roared. Janie and Brian had little foam wedges in their ears so they wouldn't go deaf and insane.

Covering his movements with his body, Brian tried to get some sandwich quarters.

Janie snatched them first. "Think I'm too tired to guard my winnings?"

And then Reeve was there, laughing. "I have sisters like that," he told Brian. "Luckily they're much older than I am and they were out of the house most of my life. Here. I saw what was going on, I brought reinforcements." He handed Brian a pack of sandwiches.

Brian checked to be sure they were good ones. He

didn't want some squashed baloney reject. Reeve had brought the best: roast beef and ham. Food to reach six feet by.

"Are we up next?" said Janie, bouncing on the cement seat, which Brian rather admired.

Reeve glowed when Janie referred to the team as *we*. "Race after next."

"I can't see you very well," said Janie crossly, "no matter where Bri and I go."

"Come back down with me," said Reeve. "You can see great from the pits."

Brian knew he was dying to show Janie off. Janie had the Spring family hair: sprawling masses of red. Even dusted with track grit, she was beautiful.

"Go on, Janie, I'll be fine," said Brian.

Look at me, he thought, helping him get Janie back.

• • •

Reeve installed Janie on a folding chair up in the truck bed so that she could watch but wasn't in the way. It was dangerous. Stock cars coming off the track whipped in and out. Crews swung wrenches and jacks and even wheels.

Janie could see only a slice of track from here, but the sound was immense. She put the foam wedges back in her ears. The dulling of sound turned her into a spectator instead of a participant; everything slid over a space. It was soothing to be slightly deaf. She watched Reeve work.

He was exceedingly dirty. He'd helped the guys in the next slot change a tire because they were short

52

a crew member. His moppy hair clung to his head in sweaty clumps and his cheeks were pink from sunburn. Streaks of grease lubricated his entire left arm. She didn't think she had ever seen anybody as handsome.

The sun burned down.

Heat and light did their usual trick. Enough of them, and you ceased to think. You just baked.

Is this what Hannah wanted? Janie wondered. To be a spectator of life? No participation? No risk?

To let the cult choose all and guide all and decide all?

And then something—but what? *What?*—turned Hannah into a kidnapper.

I wouldn't mind being a nonparticipant, thought Janie. I could lie in the sun forever and let my bones bleach.

But even if I do nothing about that folder, I am participating. The facts are still inside it. I'm not a toddler strapped in a swing. I'm more like a parachute jumper, wondering if the rip cord works.

Reeve's car, #64 painted huge and neon orange all over it, was about to enter its first race. Reeve and the crew ran alongside, escorting their car to the track. Janie stood up in the truck bed to yell "Good luck!" but over the roar of thirty cars without mufflers, nobody heard. She flung her arms over her head and did some cheerleader moves. Nobody saw. The boys on the crew were pummeling each other with delight as #64 peeled onto the track.

Lightly, she touched her paper bracelet. It was plasticized paper that would neither rip nor fade.

Among the discoveries Janie had made after she identified herself on the milk carton was that when Hannah had left home, she'd taken nothing: no bracelet, no prom corsage, no yearbook or flute. At some terrible point, Frank and Miranda had packed Hannah's belongings in trunks, which sat in the back of the attic and gathered dust.

Janie was a saver. She liked to be reminded of every good thing and every good time. If I were last seen flying west, she thought, what would I take? Would I keep a flag bracelet, to remind me of Brian and sandwiches and cars?

Or would I leave everything behind, until everything became nothing?

Reeve came running back, waving and signaling, since speech was pretty much useless during a race. When she hopped down from the truck bed, he grabbed her hand. "Can't see the race from here," he yelled. "We'll run up and sit with Brian."

She smiled and ran with him. Running was a relief. It felt like an accomplishment.

I'm not exactly in a race, Janie thought. It's more like hide-and-seek. Hannah's not quite hidden anymore. So do I seek?

• • •

It was time for the water truck to circle the track and spray the dust down. Then stock cars would pack the track, driving around and around in single file; getting muddy, spinning out, wearing a groove.

The next race wouldn't be ideal, because the surface would be damp and slippery. But soon the track would be smooth and perfect. The lucky cars in that race got the best.

Driving on dirt meant that each race changed the properties of the track. Your car didn't necessarily ever have a lap when the surface was perfect.

The pungent flat stink of engine fuel filled Reeve's nose. Janie's hair brushed his bare arms. He hoped she'd be willing to stay all evening and party with the crew when the races were over and everybody sat around shooting the breeze while they packed up generators and fire suits.

"We came in fifth," moaned Brian. "I thought we'd win."

"Fifth out of thirty is good," said Reeve. "We keep that up, we get a trophy."

There were not divided seats, just bleachers, and the top row was packed with spectators. Janie and Reeve wedged themselves in where Brian's cooler had saved a single space. Janie was in the middle.

"Speaking of trophies, Janie," said Brian, "what about Hunting Jaguars?" Brian was drugged by too much sun. He could take nothing seriously. His voice was light and teasing. "Your father is supporting endangered species? Is that it, Janie? That's why the file folder H.J. is in Paid Bills?"

Reeve's mind fixed on that word *supporting*, and suddenly he knew.

Supporting, thought Reeve. Oh, no.

No.

He felt the size of it: a betrayal as large as oceans,

making his own betrayal a mere puddle. Janie had survived Reeve's cruelty. In her father's, she might drown.

On the track, a yellow flag was up. The cars moved slowly; quietly.

Why can't Janie have a whole race when the surface is perfect? thought Reeve.

"Come on, Janie," said Brian. "Was that a checkbook in there? Is that what made you so mad?"

The yellow flag lifted.

The green flag swirled.

I can't help her, thought Reeve.

For a moment, he hated Mr. Johnson, and in that moment he felt more bound to Janie than he had by love. For her sake, he hated and he understood hate.

The cars leaped forward, and the sound of their engines was primal; gut-wrenching. They roared in circles, like Janie's life, forever back at the starting line.

Reeve did not expect Janie to answer Brian, but at the next yellow flag, when the track was relatively silent, her voice came out, dented like a fender. "My father," said Janie, "knows where my kidnapper is. I think he may always have known I was kidnapped." She was shaking from the horror of it. Frank Johnson, *knowing* this was no granddaughter; real parents were out there in an agony of fear. "In any case, he pays her bills." A quivery desperate smile worked its way to her mouth. "My father is supporting my kidnapper."

CHAPTER
SIX

Never was the word that had ruled Brian Spring.

You will *never* leave the house without permission, you will *never* speak to strangers, you will *never* take risks. You will *never* be like your sister Jennie and disappear.

Frank and Miranda Johnson had claimed—in front of the real parents; in front of the New Jersey police; the FBI; lawyers; judges—"We didn't know what Hannah did." Under oath, they had said, "We never heard from her again."

Never was their word too. We have *never* gotten in touch. We are *not* guilty.

But Frank had gotten in touch. He *was* guilty, thought Brian, his thoughts racing. Covering the tracks of a kidnapper! Mr. Johnson could probably be arrested for that. Well, probably not on his deathbed.

Besides, somebody would have to tell.

Brian wasn't telling. Janie wasn't telling.

Reeve? Would he? He'd told things before.

"I bet your mom didn't know, Janie," said Brian, working it out. "She wouldn't have let us into the office, sorting through his papers, not if she knew. But"—Brian frowned, not liking this flaw in the research process—"you're not going to be able to ask your father for details. Stroke victims. Sometimes they don't learn how to talk again."

He began speculating when and how Hannah and her father got in touch, and how much money he had given her.

Janie said nothing, while Reeve stared at his hands, but Brian was oddly excited. He was part of a team and they had a secret. *Frank Johnson knew where the kidnapper was.* Brian would go home in possession of this secret like a spy in war. It would give Brian an edge. He needed an edge.

They sat through thirty laps of another race, while little kids whose fathers were on pit crews ran up and down the bleachers, eating hot dogs and playing tag.

When the race ended, silence sat around like dust. They could taste it.

There's another edge, thought Brian. The edge Janie's standing on. She dumped our family after living with us only a few months. She waved good-bye and went back home to live with the good guys.

But she was wrong. She went home—to the bad guys.

● ● ●

58

You hollowed out your stock car when you rebuilt it for racing. Reeve's #64 was a Monte Carlo, seats removed, glass out, roll bars added, doors sealed.

Reeve felt the same.

Last winter Lizzie's law firm had had a case involving the possible laundering of drug money. And whose drug money had it been but the very cult of which Hannah had been a part? Cult records recorded Hannah's death. Lizzie had even found a death certificate on file in Los Angeles County. She'd told Reeve about it but made him promise to say nothing. It wasn't her right to reveal what she had stumbled on. The information, Lizzie explained, would eventually reach the right people in the FBI, who would notify the Johnsons that Hannah was dead.

But that never happened. The Johnsons were told no such thing.

Why not?

Lizzie did not make mistakes. It was what made her so tiresome. Made it impossible to imagine William, and how he could be in love with her. If Lizzie said Hannah was dead, then Reeve believed she was.

So who was Frank Johnson supporting?

It couldn't be Hannah.

. . . unless Hannah had faked her death.

Or the cult had faked it.

Did a cult believe that anybody who left their group to do something else *was* dead? So they filled out papers?

59

And if so, who was the person who cashed those checks Frank wrote?

Some other cult member could have stumbled across family information in yet another file, in yet another hidden drawer, and could be using it to extort money from a desperate parent!

Reeve imagined Frank Johnson endlessly paying off a fake daughter, slamming the drawer shut on his secret, joining Janie and his wife in the kitchen for a snack, smiling as if there were no lies.

"You two are so dense!" said Janie, flapping her baseball cap for emphasis, glaring first at Reeve on her right and then at Brian on her left. "I can't believe I've told you but now I *have* gone and told you and yet you don't understand *anything*!"

Reeve was exhausted. He lacked the strength for more thinking. "Your father can't talk about it, Janie. I know you're not going to tell the police. You're certainly not going to tell your mother; she can't handle another problem. She can't even put gas in the tank."

Janie slumped her shoulders, flung her mass of hair backward and then ratcheted herself up again as if she were with the two stupidest people in America.

"My mother had me go through those files for a reason," said Janie, slowly and clearly. "Remember? She wants me to handle the bills."

The boys wore the blank stretched smiles of

people who don't get it. They nodded, though, hoping Janie would see something worthy in them.

"I have to decide whether to *keep* supporting her," said Janie. "My own kidnapper."

CHAPTER
SEVEN

In moments of delight, Kathleen tended to attack.
She liked to yank so hard on Stephen's red hair he
was glad baldness didn't run in his family, or this
would start it.

"They'll be here in a minute, Stephen!" said Kathleen. "I can't wait for Dad and Mom to meet you."

He almost forgave her for choosing his clothes
and then ironing them. He could not have fallen for
a girl who shrugged about parents. Stephen's parents had held his hand (and he theirs) through so
much.

"There they are!" Kathleen was much too loud.
People turned and stared. Stephen just laughed,
enjoying her noise. Kathleen leaped away from him,
hauling open the hotel door and flinging herself all
over her parents. A dozen strangers watched and
smiled, enveloped in Kathleen's reunion.

"This," said Kathleen, hanging on to her father's

arm and beaming, "is my dad, Harry Donnelly. Dad, *this* is Stephen."

"Mr. Donnelly," said Stephen, shaking hands. "It's great to meet you."

There was not even time to let go of Mr. Donnelly's hand. Not even time to say hello to Mrs. Donnelly. It turned out there were things Kathleen had never gotten around to mentioning either. She said proudly, "Dad just does consulting now, but he was an FBI agent."

Stephen felt actual horror.

His spine lifted him up, his feet moved him backward, and his hand turned cold and stiff inside Mr. Donnelly's.

How many times had the Spring family had to deal with the FBI?

The last time Mr. Mollison, their own personal FBI agent, had come back into their lives, it had been to interrogate Janie. He had thrust her up against the living room wall, demanding details. Stephen's father had intervened; made the FBI go away and refused to let them talk to Janie again.

Stephen liked Mr. Mollison but equally loathed him, because when you had the FBI in your life, you knew your world was neither normal nor safe.

All that was safe and normal exploded for Stephen. He didn't want dinner with these people, even if they were Kathleen's parents. He could feel the past getting ready to scorch him again.

He did manage a smile for Kathleen's mother. He did follow the maitre d' to the table. He sat down without kicking anybody's chair. But he could not look at Mr. Donnelly. He knew, because he was overly familiar with police, that the man would be fully aware of his reaction. If Stephen's eyes met Mr. Donnelly's, he would not see the much-loved father of Kathleen Marie. He would see the eyes of a cop who wanted to know why.

Apparently, dinner was wonderful. Everybody else ordered exotic: buffalo sausage or venison steak. Stephen had a glorified hamburger and difficulty chewing. He knew his cheeks were smudged red from anxiety, and that Harry Donnelly would see that mark of tension.

Kathleen, less aware, said, "Gosh, it's warm in here, isn't it, Stephen? Your cheeks are as hot as if we'd just run up Flagstaff Mountain."

Stephen nodded and stirred his iced tea.

Mrs. Donnelly was a river of information about high school friends Kathleen had never mentioned. Stephen let the gossip pour over him. It was rather pleasant, hearing how Kelsey was happy at the University of Wisconsin, Josh had not failed out of UConn after all and Craig was transferring.

Stephen was letting his mind drift toward dessert, because halfway through any meal, Stephen lost interest in protein and began to think about sugar, when Mrs. Donnelly said, "Tell us about your family, Stephen. We know you have twin brothers, Brendan and Brian, and a younger sister, Jodie."

He had been with Kathleen since last October and never mentioned his second sister.

He knew that, he had intended that, but the public proof of it shocked even Stephen Spring.

If he told about Janie, he would never again be a guy Kathleen met at college. He would always be, as he was in New Jersey, a guy whose sister had been kidnapped.

But if he didn't tell, what kind of loyalty was that?

Stephen was holding his glass of tea so tightly it squeezed out the bottom of his grip like toothpaste and landed on the table.

When Janie had been at her worst—temper tantrums; stalking away from her real family so they'd let her go back to her fake one—Stephen's mother and father had ordered them to accept her behavior. No matter what, said Stephen's parents, we will go on loving her.

I want to go on lying about her, thought Stephen.

He felt like a basketball player on the free-throw line; score tied; three seconds left. Ignore the screaming crowd, the hope of victory and the fear of failure. Try to think of nothing except a little metal hoop and a little dangling string.

Stephen tried to think of nothing except his duty to his family and a few dangling lives.

"Actually," he said, fighting for control over his voice, "I have another sister. I never told you, Kath. She was kidnapped when we were little. It destroyed our lives." He pressed the icy glass against his cheek, literally trying to chill out. "She turned up a year and a half ago and the situation is crummy. I don't want to talk about it."

He drank firmly, like a punctuation mark, and Kathleen said, "What—are you nuts? Of course we're going to talk about it. Start at the beginning. Don't leave out a thing."

• • •

For Kathleen it was a soap opera, delightfully close to hand. Her interrogation took an hour. Stephen thought he had probably lost weight from the stress of it. He ordered a second dessert.

"Wow," said Kathleen, tilting back in her chair. She licked her lips as if the story had been chocolate cake. "So right now, your sister Jennie is staying Janie, keeping her kidnap name, living with her kidnap family, and you're all agreeing to this!" Kathleen shook her head. "And nobody is even rude enough to mention to the Frank and Miranda parents that their real daughter is a kidnapper?"

Stephen shrugged. It didn't come easily. There was nothing to shrug about. "Janie loves them. We knock them, we lose her again. Actually, I kind of like her parents. My little brother Brian is even spending the summer with them. It's the kidnapper we hate."

"Hannah," breathed Kathleen dramatically.

"I never call her Hannah. It's too friendly. You call her Hannah, you could let it go. I'm never letting go. If I ever found that woman, I'd get my revenge."

Kathleen frowned. "I don't think that's kind, Stephen. The poor woman is some demented loser who

66

couldn't even keep her place in a cult. She had to steal a kid to have company. Anyway, so many years have gone by."

"Not that many years." Stephen didn't have enough air to speak. His voice cracked over the thought of the years, and how they had gone by for the Springs.

"Janie didn't suffer," Kathleen pointed out.

"That doesn't matter," said her father. "His family got stabbed in the back every day of Stephen's childhood."

Mr. Donnelly sounded as if he were familiar with the Spring/Johnson nightmare. Worry slammed through Stephen. Was Mr. Donnelly just a consultant? What did he consult about? Could he be seeking information from Stephen? Could he be investigating the kidnapping?

No. It wouldn't happen this way. Kathleen couldn't have been sicced on him to get information —she wouldn't have waited since October to reach the topic.

And probably Mr. Donnelly was just familiar with kidnapping in general; had possibly handled one. But not Janie's.

It was coincidence. Stephen was overreacting. Kathleen was just a girlfriend and Mr. Donnelly was just her dad. Nothing was going to split open.

His head hurt so much that he wanted a bandage to wind around his jaw and up over his hair.

"If I were Miranda Johnson," said Mrs. Donnelly, "and I found out that my daughter did what Hannah did, I'd kill myself."

Stephen nodded. He thought Mr. Johnson sort of had.

"Did you ever try to find the Javensen woman?" asked Mr. Donnelly.

He's just curious, Stephen told himself. Get this over with. "Once," he admitted. "The police thought she might have been in New York, so my sister Jodie and I actually went into the city and started walking. We thought we could spot her." He flushed at the childishness of it. "I thought she'd eat at a soup kitchen, and we could show her photograph around and people would tell us where she lived."

"That's actually a pretty good approach," said Mr. Donnelly.

"Will you try again?" asked Kathleen's mother.

"If I hunt her down," Stephen said slowly, "I'm letting the woman rule my life again. I won't do that. But if I stumbled on a clue, I'd follow through. I'd want a trial. I'd want her declared guilty. I'd want her in prison."

But this was a lie.

To have the past back?

It would destroy him.

CHAPTER
EIGHT

Back when Janie had discovered the milk carton, which she flattened and hid and slipped out ten times a day to see if it was still her face on there— and it was—she had pictured the Spring family in New Jersey lurking in the bushes of her life. Waiting to leap out and drag her away.

But no.

It was Hannah leaping out. Hannah with the power to control Janie no matter how many years went by.

Janie and Reeve and Brian didn't stay for the race parties, even though #64 placed in three races. Reeve came home with Janie and Brian. Nobody talked much until they reached the house and saw that Mrs. Johnson's car was not in the driveway. There was nobody home.

The boys followed Janie inside. Everybody had something cold to drink.

Janie rinsed her glass in the sink, letting hot tap

water soothe her trembling hands. Brian and Reeve were thinking about money and payments and the FBI. She was thinking about Honor thy father and mother.

Did I pick the wrong pair to honor? Should I have stayed in New Jersey and become Jennie Spring again, and let Frank and Miranda Johnson sink into the past?

She had gotten to know her blood parents as you know relatives you see on holidays: comfortably, but not well.

Maybe you never knew anybody well.

Could she trust Brian and Reeve? She almost laughed. It was ridiculous to worry about trust when the contents of the folder proved there was no such thing. "I'm going to go through the file," she told them. "You can come if you want."

They came.

The little office was hot and musty.

Only a few years earlier, Janie had learned keyboarding on a typewriter. Now the high school had four hundred computers. Janie could type her birth name on one of those computers and read about herself on the Internet. She felt unsafe online, as if some site might burst open and the face of Hannah Javensen would stare out at her, mocking.

Janie touched the handle of the Paid Bills drawer. Hannah had been right here in the house with her, hiding in the back of a dark desk.

They sat on the floor, backs against the wall, Janie in the middle, exactly as they had at the races, and she opened the file and held it so that they could read together.

Except that Janie could not seem to read.

She could see rows of little black print on the pages she was turning, but she could not decipher them. It was almost funny. Here was every piece of information her father had gathered, and she had lost the ability to read.

Do I trust Reeve? On a basic level, I do. He's not going to steal the silver. But eclipse level? Guide-me-through-the-dark trust?

I don't even know how to define the word *trust*. It's one of those gut words, like *faith* and *honor*. If you have it, you know it.

But Reeve can read and he can think, and I can't do either one. So forget trust, just be practical and ask for help.

When she could speak without sobbing, she said, "So what's your conclusion about this stuff, Reeve?"

• • •

Reeve was afraid for her. She was as stiff as an angle iron, not so much sitting next to him as welded to the wall and the floor. One by one, she turned over the check stubs and paid bills and miscellaneous paperwork, but her eyes seemed stuck out beyond the words, and he knew she was not reading.

She handed him the file, which surprised him, but he took over, sorting the papers into piles. It was remarkable how old bills could tell a story. And what also surprised him was how simple it was. It was just barely a mystery.

71

"Frank didn't hire a private detective to find Hannah," said Reeve finally. "He did the same thing your family did, Brian. He kept his old phone number. Probably had a recording for Hannah. Like— *Mother and Dad love you. Tell us how to reach you.*"

Reeve had a hideous vision of a father calling in to that machine, month after month, year after year, hoping for the voice of his lost daughter.

Janie's left hand lay like a cold paperweight on top of the papers they'd already looked at, while her right hand fluttered nervously around her face. Reeve wondered if he could take Janie's hand and decided he couldn't.

"The bank Frank uses is in Atlanta. His name is printed on the checks, but no address and no phone, so Hannah can't locate him through the checks. Frank doesn't want to see her or hear from her, I guess; he just wants her to have money." He nudged Janie. "Look at this, this is important, this is good." He stabbed a page with his finger, but Janie did not look down.

"Janie, listen to me! This is good. Frank *hasn't* always known where Hannah is. He doesn't start sending money until three and a half years ago. He finds her, or else she calls in, or something happens."

They all knew what had happened three and a half years ago. Nobody said it out loud.

"From then on," said Reeve, studying the entries, "he sends money four times a year."

The large amount of money in the account was

puzzling. Why so much? Cuts down on how often he has to think about it, Reeve decided. He has to write checks, but at least he doesn't have to make deposits.

Next Reeve picked up the police report. Brian read along avidly, but Janie turned her face away. She wants the old version, thought Reeve, the one that doesn't work anymore.

"How do you think Frank got hold of that report, Reeve?" asked Brian. "Do you think he stole it from the police? Do you think when their backs were turned, he snatched it up?"

"He probably just asked." Reeve thought of the poor guy lying and faking in front of New York police. "There are two police reports. The older one is her arrest for—" He stopped himself. "Is her arrest. Going by the dates on the checks, I'm going to guess that when they released her, she tried her old phone number for the first time. She got Frank's machine and a few weeks later, Frank begins to support her."

"She's so vicious!" cried Janie. "So rotten!" She pressed her fingers together steeple style, so hard Reeve was afraid she would snap them backward and they'd be picking fingers up off the floor.

"All those years," whispered Janie, "and Hannah doesn't bother with her family. Not on their birthdays. Not on their anniversary. Not Christmas. But she gets arrested as a prostitute and calls up her father."

Reeve pictured Frank checking for messages and

73

hearing that one. How could that feel? What if Reeve had to find that out about one of his sisters, or his cousins—or Janie?

It would kill you.

The Johnsons lived in Connecticut a couple of hours north of New York City. Had Frank driven in? Picked Hannah up? Taken her to the airport? Bought her that ticket? Told her to change her name from Javensen to Johnson too, so that she could vanish?

Oh, thought Reeve, weak with relief. She *can't* be an impostor. Frank met her. He *could* have gotten the plane ticket with a credit card and wired money, but I bet he didn't. I bet he had to see her.

Had Frank brought pictures of Janie to show off? Had he said, Do you want to see how your little girl turned out?

No, he wouldn't dare. Pictures might tempt Hannah to stay. Frank would want Hannah to get on the plane and go.

But what would Hannah have answered, anyway? Would she have frowned in confusion? (What kid? Oh, you mean the one I kidnapped and left with you? I forgot about her.)

Hannah's form of evil was forgetfulness. She forgot to be kind, she forgot to be thoughtful. She forgot her parents. How terrible, how sad, that she'd remembered her old phone number, and that it had still been connected.

Reeve watched Janie press her palms against the floor on either side of her, and now it was her elbows and wrists that Reeve had to worry about, as she seemed perfectly willing to snap those off.

"I bet she didn't even say, *How are you?*" cried Janie. "I bet she didn't even say, *I'm sorry.* I bet she didn't say, *So how's your life been?* I bet she said, *Bring money.*"

Janie wrapped her arms tightly around herself, as if to squeeze all the blood out of her heart.

Reeve's eyes met Brian's. We don't dare touch her, he thought. Helpless, he went on through the folder.

"Look, Janie," he said, deeply relieved. "Right here. Truly good news. Look at the date the phone bills stop. It's the month Lizzie figures out who you really are and what really happened. Frank thinks Hannah is your mother and you're his granddaughter right up to the minute when Lizzie walks into the house and tells him about your face on the milk carton. That's the first minute he knows about the kidnapping, Janie. And what does he do? He cancels the phone. He keeps sending money, he can't abandon her entirely, but he doesn't give Hannah a way to reach him again."

Truly good news, Reeve had just said. But it was not good news. Not for Frank Johnson.

On that stub was recorded the moment in which a father knew he would never speak to his daughter again. He had been tricked and lied to, but far worse, his belief that he was a great father to Janie had been brutally destroyed.

He was no father.

He was part of a kidnapping.

● ● ●

On her father's desk were bookends Janie had made in Brownies. The girls had split their own geodes and glued them to L-shaped pieces of wood, which they had cut, notched and polished. When she'd given them to Dad, Janie thought they were the most beautiful bookends in the world. From here, she saw they were not level and not smooth; they were poorly stained, and missing one geode. Why keep them?

But she knew why Frank Johnson had kept those bookends.

There was only one reason in the world to keep bookends or an old telephone number. Only one reason in the world to send money to a lost child. Only one reason to protect Hannah.

Love.

He loved Hannah.

For a dizzying moment, Janie felt herself back at the races, high on the bleachers, while cars flew around an egg-shaped track, drying out the spray from the water truck.

Water evaporated.

Parental love did not.

The child grows up, does wrong things, stupid things, and the father still loves her. And no matter what, the father cannot bear her suffering. And so the father endlessly tries to help.

Love went on.

Oh, Daddy! she thought. I understand love. My New Jersey mother kept loving me when I was missing, and when I was found she loved me enough to let me go. So I know what love is, Daddy. I know you loved Hannah. "But what about me, Daddy? I'm not mad at you anymore, but what am I supposed to do?"

She hadn't meant to speak out loud, but out it came, in such pain that both boys hugged her at the same time and everybody's arms bumped.

Janie wept.

Reeve reached up with his sneaker tip and knocked a box of Kleenex off Mrs. Johnson's desk and onto the floor. Brian hooked it with his sneaker. They kicked it up into their laps without letting go of each other, and the three of them watched its slow progress. Janie took a handful of tissues.

"Why do you have to do anything?" asked Brian. "Just pretend you didn't find the file."

"The day on which the check is written is coming up, Brian. Do I send Hannah money? Or do I not send Hannah money?"

"That's easy. You don't. The woman killed our family. You can't go and send her money so she can eat out and have cable TV. Let her starve. Let her live in a gutter."

"But Brian," said Janie, "that's the point. She *might* go live in a gutter. Remember why she was arrested. She was a hooker. A person nobody ever wants his own kid to become. What if, without Frank's money, she'd be back on the street? What do I owe my father? Do I owe it to him to keep supporting his daughter? She's his real daughter, Brian. I'm just passing through."

77

• • •

It was Brian who decided they needed chocolate. He got up off the floor, offering to make everybody a sundae.

"Heat the chocolate sauce," said Reeve.

"You go with him," Janie said, pushing him gently. "You heat the chocolate sauce."

Reeve opened his mouth to protest.

"I need to pull myself together," she said.

He almost didn't go, so she looked away from him, and frowned down into the folder, and he was forced to follow Brian into the kitchen.

She had said it out loud to a brother and an ex-boyfriend, the worst thought of all: I'm not the daughter who counts.

She hoped she could trust them. There was no way to pretend she had not said those words.

Janie put every paper neatly back into the folder. Clumsily getting to her knees, with her right hand she found the alphabetical space for H. J. and with her left shifted the folder to the proper angle for inserting it into the drawer, and there, on the back outside of the heavy paper, was a lightly penciled address.

A post office box, a city and state.

Of course.

The checks had to be mailed.

The kidnapper lived someplace. She was not just out there, adrift in a population of two hundred fifty million.

She isn't lost, thought Janie, staring in horror

78

and fascination at the address. Frank is lost. But Hannah is *there*. In Boulder, Colorado. Where Stephen is.

Janie Johnson took a deep breath.

I could go.

I could visit Stephen.

And find Hannah.

CHAPTER
NINE

"I'm home!" called Janie's mother.

Janie closed the file drawer.

From the kitchen drifted voices and the rich sweet smell of chocolate.

"Hi, Mrs. Johnson," said Reeve. "How's Mr. Johnson? Any better?"

"He is. I truly believe he squeezed my hand."

"That's great," said Brian. "We should celebrate. We're all having chocolate sundaes. You want chocolate or cookie dough ice cream with yours, Mrs. J.?"

Janie slipped through the hall and ran lightly up the stairs to her room. Now that the boys had proved how easily they could read her face, she needed to stand in private until her face got slack and boring. The boys thought they knew everything.

They knew nothing.

In the mirror she saw that her eyes had flared too wide and her cheeks sported hot pink blotches. She opened a bottle of lotion and rubbed it over her face and into her skin. She stretched her arms and shook her wrists, then shook her shoulders, waist, hips, knees and ankles, to the tune of an old elementary school gym song.

Then she emptied her lungs, as if the room were full of birthday candles and she must puff out hundreds.

Find Hannah.

Ask the thousand questions that had stung Janie like wasps since the day she first saw her face on the milk carton. Why? *Why me?* What made you do it? How did you do it? Did I laugh? Did I mind being stolen from my family? When you thought my name was Janie, not Jennie, did I argue? Did I cry? Did you slap me?

And afterward.

Oh, Hannah, afterward.

When you saw your mother and father for the first time in years, and lied to them, saying, "This is your granddaughter," were you laughing at them? Taking some obscure revenge? Or was it just convenient?

What were you running from? What were you running toward?

Why did you take me with you? Why didn't you take me the rest of the way? Where did you go next?

Did you think about that family in New Jersey, and what they would go through when their baby vanished? Did you think about them every night? Did you have nightmares?

Or did you forget?

All those years, Hannah!

Where have you been? What have you been doing? Have you ever loved? Or do you still use people, throw them away, and drive on?

She found that she was kneading lotion into her hands like a surgeon scrubbing.

I can find her, Janie thought. It won't be hard. She gets money four times a year, and that date is coming up. If you get money only every three months, you're not going to forget about showing up at the post office. You'll be there on time. So I mail her check to that box, and then I wait at the post office!

She ran a movie of this through her mind and saw herself standing around for hours, or days, hoping to spot a Hannah-like adult.

It wouldn't work.

Janie paced, circling her bed, rearranging pillows as if they were Hannah's throat.

I know. Instead of putting the check in the envelope, *I'll put in a note.* I'll tell her to meet me someplace and she'll get her money after we talk.

Yes!

But how sick. How scary.

Writing a letter to my kidnapper.

Handwriting was so intimate. It was impossible. She would have to do it on the computer and print it out. But even then—write to this person who had mutilated their lives?

But kidnapping, too, possessed a terrible intimacy. Janie had no real memory because she'd been so little. But Hannah Javensen would remember.

82

I'm doing it, Janie thought fiercely. I'll get a guide-book and figure out a good spot to meet Hannah.

Her body was a race car. Every physiological count rocketed—pulse, temperature, adrenaline—her thoughts roaring, leaping, slamming into the dark cold night of finding Hannah Javensen.

All she had to do was visit Stephen. Soon.

He's bound to be in class or at work during the day, Janie thought, so I'll have lots of time on my own. Time to scout out—

"Janie!" called her mother from the bottom of the stairs. "Sundaes are ready! Chocolate is hot, ice cream is cold!"

Janie knew what she would see when she reached the stair landing. Her mother—silvery haired; rings swinging loose on her fingers because she had lost so much weight—would be beautifully dressed, probably in a suit: a long slim jacket, a bright silk blouse, a beautifully tied scarf and pin. She would be looking up the stairs, ready to smile.

Miranda Johnson must not have an inkling of Janie's plans. Neither must Reeve. Certainly not Brian.

Let them think she was worried and heartsick be-cause her father wrote a check now and then. Don't let them figure out that she had a way to reach her kidnapper by herself.

I must have no expression on my face, Janie told herself, except pleasure at the taste of chocolate. "Coming!" she called.

• • •

In the kitchen Janie accepted her sundae, sat in her chair at the old oak table opposite Reeve and managed to hang on to her spoon without flipping it through a window or up at the ceiling.

Every muscle and joint in her body twitched, as if her intent were to run all the way to Colorado. She wanted to leap up on the table and tap-dance, trampoline, do acrobatics. "No, thank you, Brian," she said politely, "no marshmallow sauce."

Her mother was saying, "Fifth! Reeve, that's wonderful. Are you going to become a driver, do you think, or stay on as pit crew? I don't think I want you to drive. It's quite dangerous, isn't it? How fast do they really go?"

Reeve lied about how fast they really went. His lies were comforting and sane and reasonable. But they were still lies.

Janie marshaled her own lying powers. Her father was relatively stable right now, and she could probably convince Mom that she, Janie, required a rest and a change of pace. That part probably wouldn't be hard.

The hard part was coming up with a reason to visit Stephen.

He's my brother? I love him? I miss him?

No, because she and Stephen had despised each other during her short life as Jennie Spring last year. He'd thought she was a spoiled brat, and when she returned to Connecticut as Janie Johnson, he'd said that proved his point. Janie had acknowledged a certain amount of spoiled brattage in herself and when Stephen was home over Thanksgiving and

Christmas, had admitted it to him. They'd actually gotten along—for two days.

How about this? she thought. I want to go to college in Colorado. Every Connecticut teenager goes through a Colorado stage. Mine just began. What better way to decide on a school? Go and stay with Stephen.

Mom won't let me stay in his actual room but Stephen must know some girls, and I can stay in their room. Or in a hotel.

Okay. Would Stephen say yes? He might not. Stephen was difficult at best. And his best did not show up that often. Stephen was outstanding at being his worst.

What if he said no?

She had to think of a way to do this so that he'd jump at the chance to have her.

Brian.

She would use Brian.

Brian adored Stephen, and missed him terribly, and often compared him to Reeve, which Janie did not think was fair to either of them. She would say to Brian, I want to go to the university in Boulder, like Stephen, and of course I need to see the campus and talk to people, and why don't you and I fly out to Boulder for a few days?

Her New Jersey parents would go all warm and cuddly at the idea of their two sons united out West and in the presence of the lost sister. They'd be thrilled that Janie wanted to go to school where Stephen was; automatic big-brother care would be part of the college package.

Nobody would consult Stephen; they knew better. Stephen didn't do care packages.

The lies were shaping up well.

Once they were in Boulder, she would suggest brotherly activities; Brian and Stephen must hike, or white-water raft, or whatever they did out there.

She, Janie, would be hunting.

CHAPTER
TEN

The following morning, the weather was dull and gray.

Brian sat with his book on the Trojan War open to an illustration from a vase painting: Achilles fighting Hector, orange on black. They were immense men, with great jarring rectangular muscles and fierce jutting chins.

Janie's voice, bright and quick as a chipmunk, spattered at him.

Did she always sound like that?

Brian tried to think clearly.

Hardly anybody in the Trojan War tried to think clearly. They just slaughtered each other. Brian, however, liked to be clear. He liked his facts orderly, and chronological, and carefully laid out.

"But Janie, you've always wanted to go to UConn," he said, "so that you'd be only an hour's drive from your parents. Colorado is two thousand miles away. And you and Stephen don't get along all that well."

"But don't you want to visit him?" said Janie.

"I'd love to," said Brian uneasily.

Last night, she'd been seething. Calling the kidnapper vicious and rotten. Drenched with tears, using up half a box of Kleenex. She'd been shouting and slamming her hands on the floor.

Now all she wanted was a few days' rest in Colorado? Since when had Stephen ever been restful?

And why was she talking in this cheery little voice?

"But you're right," he said slowly, "that Mom and Dad will say yes. They've really loosened up this year."

Not only was Jodie already packing for college, Mom herself had gone back to school, taking a full summer semester along with working. Dad had started traveling for his job, which he never used to do, fearful of being away from the kids. Kidnap fear had been set to rest, and Dad was thrilled with his travel, with the being-away time, no need to check on each child before he made a move. But while Brendan was going to sport camps, Brian was just filling time with Janie's kidnap family. Brian knew his parents would let him go anywhere.

He watched Janie carefully. Then he said, "I'm not sure Stephen wants us out there. He's kind of separated himself, you know. Dad says it's a way to leave the kidnapping behind."

Janie did not seem to care whether Stephen wanted them or not. "I'd wander around the campus," she said airily. "Have an interview, check things out. You and Stephen would have adventures together. You know. Backpacking. Canoeing."

"I only like to read about adventure," said Brian. He tried to figure out a connection between the file folder and this giddy travelogue, but he couldn't come up with anything. "And Stephen's working full time plus going to class; he can't fit that in."

But how he'd love to visit Stephen. He'd never been west and he'd only flown twice. To cross the Great Plains! See the Rocky Mountains!

Already Brian was losing interest in the Trojan War and wondering where he had put his *Journals of Lewis and Clark*.

"Please, Brian?" coaxed Janie. "Call Stephen for me?"

Brian turned pages as if he might find a clue in the history of Troy. Finally, unwillingly, he said, "Did you find something else in that folder after Reeve and I went to make sundaes?"

"Don't be silly!" Janie tilted her head from side to side like a robin wondering whether to sing or eat. "Of course I didn't. You saw everything in it, Brian. Everything. No, I've put that behind me. I think a trip out West would be such fun. Think how relaxing it would be. And you and I deserve a rest."

"What did you find?" said Brian.

Janie reached for her hair, a nervous habit she was not aware of, gripping the entire red bush in one hand and making a topknot with which she dusted her forehead.

"If you lie, I'm not calling Stephen," said Brian.

"I'll call Stephen only when you tell me what else was in the folder."

• • •

Brian reminded Janie of Lizzie. Brian and Lizzie were both really smart. Really quick. Plain basic types like Janie and Reeve could always get cornered.

She didn't have time for this.

All kinds of things threatened to trap her.

Her father's illness: He was stable right now. Tomorrow she could say, I need a break; and her mother would say, Yes, you do, darling.

But if her father got worse—and the only thing worse was death—Janie wasn't going anywhere. And if he got better—

Janie shivered at the thought of her father getting better. If he could talk, she would have to ask. She didn't want answers from *him* this time.

She wanted answers from the source.

Hannah.

And Lizzie's wedding was coming up; Janie could not be away for the wedding. Nobody would *let* her be away for the wedding.

And the date on which the check was to be written was coming up, and this was the time H. J. would be getting hungry. Perhaps literally hungry. Perhaps desperate and angry and frantic for that money.

Janie didn't want Brian to be anything but her passport to Boulder. She hoped for a timely interruption: a phone call, a mother returning, Lizzie with fabric scraps.

But nothing happened.

Nothing except that Brian really was smart. Probably one day he would be a law partner in Lizzie's firm, and together they would destroy whole corporations. Brian closed his book, changed his position and looked hard into her eyes. "I did wonder about something, Janie. The checks have to be mailed. Is the address in there? Do you know where Hannah lives now?"

Janie tried to look blank.

"Is it Colorado?" said Brian.

Janie let go of her hair. She let go of her sparkle. She said, "Boulder. Hannah Javensen has a post office box in Boulder."

• • •

Brian was glad he was sitting. Glad Janie was so busy with her hair.

The kidnapper in Boulder.

How grotesque, how sickening, that all unknowing, Stephen had been near her, breathing her same air, all these months.

The air in Brian's lungs felt filled with fungus and fever, as if Hannah had infected him.

Again he struggled for clear thought.

Back when Brian's family had first learned that a woman named Hannah Javensen had stolen Jennie, they were told that Hannah had been in a dangerous cult.

Brian, of course, had gone straight to the library to read everything he could find about cults. A cult, it turned out, was a group of people with a job: Get a victim. Drain the personality. Siphon off the soul. Keep the body for your own use.

If Hannah was still in a cult, it was truly dangerous to be in touch with her. A cult's mission stayed the same: Suck those kids in. *Keep them.* He and Janie must not get near her.

On the other hand, Hannah could have become part of ordinary society. It was possible that she had a job where no history or Social Security number was required. She might just be a person who watched her favorite TV shows and brushed her teeth, walked the dog and liked Chinese restaurants.

But she might not be.

And no matter what, Brian didn't want anything touching Stephen. "What are you going to do?" he said thickly. "Stake out the post office box?"

"I'm just going to look," said Janie.

"There's no such thing as just looking. We find her, we'll end up talking to her."

Janie hid behind her hair.

"Your father made absolutely sure Hannah couldn't know where you live, Janie. He sent all that money from a distance! Changed his name—even changed *her* name. He doesn't want anybody to be in touch. We have to trust his judgment."

This, Brian realized immediately, was ridiculous. The fact that the file existed proved that Frank had lousy judgment.

"I'm not three years old this time," said Janie. "Hannah can't take me for another ride. I want answers. I'm getting them."

"So you are going to talk to her."

"Of course not, I told you, I just want to see her."

"You're lying. You want to talk to her. I can't let you. It's dangerous. It's wrong."

Brian's life was built on being the good guy. The son who helped his mother shop and his father change the oil; the brother who softened family fights; the classmate who, when somebody asked a particularly stupid question, rephrased it so that the teacher would answer kindly and nobody would laugh.

Finding Hannah was not the act of a good guy. The only good thing about Hannah was that she was not in their lives.

He said, "I'm telling." The two words made him feel little and stupid and helpless.

"Like who?" said Janie. Her voice was hard and thin, like brittle cracker. "You can't tell my father, he's in a coma. You can't tell my mother, she'll fall apart. You can't tell your mother and father, they're too thrilled with their new lives. If they're forced to face a real live Hannah and a real live trial, their new lives are down the tube. You can't tell Stephen, he'd be first on the phone to the FBI. There's nobody to tell, Brian."

"A million things could go wrong," he protested.

"She's just some middle-aged wreck of a woman who probably can't even bag groceries."

"Then why bother?" shouted Brian. He flung the

93

book across the room, and that was rare for him; he didn't have much of a temper. He wasn't sure whether he was angry or afraid.

"This is my life Hannah took and threw off the cliff," Janie shouted back. "I have the right to close in on her. You promised you'd call Stephen if I told you what else was in that folder. I told you. So are you going to call him?"

There were so many ways in which this could explode. He had to stop her. They would all slide off the cliff again, and Hannah was the type to escape and stand at the top laughing while the others fell.

"I'm telling," said Brian.

"There's nobody to tell!" said his sister.

"Reeve. I'm telling Reeve."

CHAPTER
ELEVEN

When she was surprised, Reeve's grandmother would say, "I'm floored!"

Now Reeve knew what it meant. He felt as if Janie had used a martial arts hold and thrown him flat on the floor of Mr. Johnson's office.

What was this insanity? Meeting her own kidnapper? By herself? In a strange town?

"Just looking" was not worth a trip to Colorado. Anyway, if she "just looked" at middle-aged women who had post office boxes, how could she be sure she had the right one? She wasn't just looking. Of course she meant to talk to Hannah.

"Janie," he said, incredulous, "you can't do that. Hannah's off-limits. Finding her is a really crummy idea."

Actually, it was a really exciting idea. Hunting Hannah down would be like racing: Janie was pressing her foot to the floor, and nobody loved speed and danger more than Reeve. But this was out of the question.

"I can handle it," said Janie.

"But what if something goes wrong?"

"What could go wrong? I'm just going to look at her. She won't know who I am."

"That's not a good enough reason to fly to Colorado," said Reeve. How could Janie be this stupid? "If you want her to have money, mail it to her. What's looking going to accomplish?"

"Okay, fine. I *am* going to talk to Hannah. When she picks up her check, I'll be waiting."

Reeve was appalled. "But what would you say to her?"

"*She's* the one who's going to say things. I'll be the one listening. I want to know what happened."

"We know what happened," said Reeve irritably. "Forget your dumb questions. What if Hannah wants to come home with you or something? What if she wants to be at her father's hospital bed? What's your mother supposed to do when her criminal daughter shows up? Janie, don't be selfish."

"I'll do what I want!" she snapped.

He stared at her. This is Janie? he thought. Sweet good Janie?

She read his thoughts. "I am sick sick *sick* of being the good guy! I want to know what happened. I want to look into her eyes. I want answers."

"Janie, there aren't any questions left," said Brian.

"You don't have any questions?" said Janie to her

brother. "You don't want to know *why*? Why *me*? Why *us*? Why that afternoon? Where was she going? Why didn't she take me the rest of the way? What did she think would happen to you guys? To your mother and father? What was worth the risk? What was the plan? You don't want to ask any of that?"

Oh, Janie, thought Reeve. None of the answers could be good.

So, Frank, he thought dully, what was your point —keeping that file? You had to know that one day somebody else would read it. What was *your* plan, Frank?

But this was a nightmare without a plan. It was a Slinky on a staircase, curling down to the bottom, nobody stopping it.

Brian was correct, of course. Any one phone call to any one adult would stop it.

But Brian was also correct that the four parents couldn't and shouldn't have to endure anything more.

My parents? Reeve wondered. They're pretty immersed in Lizzie's wedding and anyway, if I asked for their help, they'd dial 911. There's Lizzie herself, but she'd just call Mr. Mollison. Once the FBI finds out, everyone we need to protect is exposed.

"There are laws," he said confusedly. "About checking accounts." Reeve didn't have one. He wasn't sure of himself. "You can't write a check on your father's account, Janie."

"Yes, I can." She was feverish with her plan. "I

97

have my parents' power of attorney. It's a legal form you fill out at the lawyer's office. It decrees that if a person is incapacitated, you take over."

This didn't sound right to Reeve. Janie was a minor. Could you grant such power to a kid? Your own kid? Or, actually, in this convoluted case, somebody else's kid you were just pretending was yours?

Practically speaking, though, Janie could write checks on that account whether it was legal or not. At a bank with a million customers, who would compare signatures? Nobody. Ever.

"I'm going to Boulder," said Janie.

"You can't get in your kidnapper's path a *second* time," said Reeve.

"I'm going."

Lord, it's only been six months since the last time I was a total jerk, thought Reeve. Am I going to be a total jerk again? Or is it Janie who's the jerk, and I'm just along for the ride?

I have to go too, and keep Janie safe while she hunts Hannah.

Hunt. A word for a wren snatched by a hawk; a chipmunk savaged by a weasel. Janie was going to hunt Hannah down. Hannah was prey.

But she deserves that, thought Reeve dizzily. Hannah is a predator herself. "Then we're all going," he said decisively. "All three of us. I'll be the one who wants to go to school in Colorado. Brian will be the one who misses his brother. You'll be the one whose father was on his deathbed, but they're talking about moving him to a rehab center and you need a break. And when we get there, you're not approaching Hannah, Janie. Promise."

I'm as crazy as she is, thought Reeve. I'm not only going along with her, I'm presenting the format! The Springs would be wild at the idea of Brian in the same town with the kidnapper, let alone the same room and the same conversation.

Well, I just won't let him out of my sight. Or Janie either.

"Then it's settled," said Janie. "Brian, you call Stephen. He has to set this up. My mother will let me go as long as Stephen finds a bed for me in a girls' dorm or something."

"Do we tell Stephen what we're doing?" asked Reeve. He liked Stephen. He didn't think anybody had told Stephen how rotten Reeve had been last year. It would be nice if Stephen had no knowledge of Reeve's flaws.

Well, Stephen would consider it a real flaw that Reeve was actually helping Janie do this. *And* letting Brian be part of it.

"We don't tell Stephen," said Brian. "He gets mad too fast."

"We have to be back in time for Lizzie's wedding," said Reeve.

There was a wall calendar in the office, but the page hadn't been flipped to July, because the owner of the calendar no longer knew what month or year it was. Janie ripped June off the pad. They studied July.

"We have time," she said. "We have ten days to put this together and get it done."

Brian telephoned Stephen.

• • •

Stephen had just come from a class discussion in which several students believed that the right cup of herbal tea would save them from pain and sorrow. Well acquainted with pain and sorrow, Stephen did not contribute to the discussion. He merely crossed these idiots off his list of possible friends.

He walked in the door of his dorm room to find the phone ringing: his little brother, asking to come visit. Asking to bring Janie and her boyfriend, Reeve.

The sweetness of it! The innocence.

A kid wanting his big brother.

"Yes!" said Stephen, laughing out loud, he was so pleased. Brian wanted to see him so much he'd coaxed Janie to pretend she wanted to attend the university. And Reeve, whom Stephen liked a lot, really did want to transfer to Boulder.

Would that be cool or what? thought Stephen.

He had a girlfriend. Now there'd be a guy to hang out with. No explanations of his history would be required. Reeve knew everything.

"This is perfect," said Stephen. "There's a ton of room in the dorms this summer. You and Reeve bunk with me, Bri, and Janie will stay with my girlfriend." Stephen ached to throw his arms around Brian, and talk, and ease his heart about Brian's failed twinship.

"You have a girlfriend?" said Brian. "You never told us."

"I'm not going to tell you now either. Don't tell Mom and Dad, don't tell Jodie, don't tell Bren."

"Why not?" said Brian. "Mom and Dad would be thrilled. Unless she's some disgusting skank leading you down a sick and twisted path."

Stephen just laughed. "You'll like her. It's just easier to separate lives. I've separated mine, okay? There's New Jersey, there's Colorado, I don't want overlap."

"I'll never tell, Stephen," said Brian very seriously, and Stephen remembered how Brian adored him. Until that moment, he had not known that his summer was empty, because it was filled with Kathleen. Now he wanted his brother and sister fiercely. That the best thing they could think of to do with their summer was to visit him!

"Let me talk to Janie," he said to Brian. I'll make it up to Janie that I never mentioned her all year, he told himself. I'll make Kathleen swear never to tell Janie I left her out.

His sister's voice was so eager. "Stephen? Is this really okay? Are you going to be glad to see us? We won't come if we're a nuisance."

"It's wonderful, Janie." For the first time, he was okay calling her by her kidnap name. She was fully Janie Johnson, not at all Jennie Spring, and that was fine.

"When are you coming?" said Stephen. Already, he could hardly wait.

CHAPTER
TWELVE

"Dad?" said Kathleen. "Did you call around? How much is true? What else did you find out?" Her voice was bright and fascinated.

True crime *was* fascinating. Unless it was yours.

Harry Donnelly had known his daughter would telephone, expecting inside information on the outrageous story of Jennie/Janie.

If anything, Stephen Spring had downplayed the drama. Every episode in the life of Jennie Spring/Janie Johnson was tragic. But more appalling, to the father of Kathleen, was the mental condition her boyfriend was in. People did not easily recover from such trauma. Some people did not recover at all. The last thing Harry Donnelly wanted was his daughter taking on some emotional wreck.

Kathleen liked people who laughed and took it easy. What was she doing falling in love with a kid who didn't laugh and wasn't easy? Trying to save him?

Nuts.

Harry Donnelly didn't care whether Stephen got saved and learned to laugh. He wanted Kathleen out of this relationship.

"Stephen did not exaggerate," he told his daughter. "He left out a lot, probably because it hurts. I'm sure he knows all of it."

Harry Donnelly was not sure of that. There was one fact Stephen Spring, and presumably his parents, had never been told. Harry Donnelly was not going to tell Kathleen, either.

The kidnapper had been arrested in New York City but released because it was before Janie had revealed herself. When Janie turned up, police checked nationwide arrest records for the name Hannah Javensen, and the New York arrest was linked up. Investigators found that Javensen had flown out of New York the day after her release from jail.

There were two interesting details in that. When she was released from jail, the woman had no money. So who had paid for the plane ticket? A ticket bought on the day of travel was expensive.

The cult had fallen on hard times and dispersed to avoid arrest for drug dealing. They'd have no use for some middle-aged woman who was broke and in trouble. Harry Donnelly doubted very much that the cult had suddenly provided an expensive plane ticket.

The likely providers of such a gift were her parents.

The other interesting detail was that Hannah

Javensen's flight had not been direct to Los Angeles. It had had a stopover in Denver.

How easy, how logical, for her to drift toward Boulder. Boulder was one of several beautiful towns in the United States, in various climates, at various elevations, that had become a haven for the ditzy, the confused, the extreme, the all-too-relaxed.

People on the edge loved Boulder.

In the midst of this pretty university town, this sophisticated little city, were so many fringe people. What better town for an ex–cult member, on the lam from every possible law enforcement agency, to live in? She'd be in a population that was comfortable evading the law. A crowd with no taste for responsibility. Doing their own thing, not worrying where the chips might fall.

Stephen was a chip. He had fallen hard. The bruises still showed.

Harry Donnelly did not think Stephen had chosen the University of Colorado because he knew about Hannah's flight plans. Stephen wouldn't have been hanging around with Kathleen if he'd thought he could be ferreting out the kidnapper.

It was claimed that in the age of the Internet, anybody could be traced easily. But this was not true. If a person decided to get along without a Social Security number (which meant: without a traditional job) and without a driver's license, or credit cards, or a phone, the path for tracing didn't exist.

Harry Donnelly had easily established that if Hannah Javensen was in Boulder, she had no phone, no credit cards and no driver's license. He'd checked under the name Johnson, too. There was nothing.

Suppose the Javensen woman had stumbled on another underground, similar to the one she had occupied in California. If this had happened—and Boulder was the place for it—only astonishing luck would bring her to the surface . . . the kind of astonishing luck that had led Janie Johnson to realize that the picture of Jennie Spring was her picture.

Luck existed.

But if Hannah Javensen materialized, Harry Donnelly wanted Kathleen in another state. "We liked Stephen, Kath," he told her, and this was true; he had liked Stephen a lot. He just didn't want the kid around anymore.

Kathleen easily switched to the topic of Stephen's virtues. She began listing for her father the wonderful things about Stephen Spring.

He said, "Kath, I'm going to be in Colorado again next week. Would it be too much to see your old dad twice in one month?"

A lifetime in law enforcement had taught him that half the battle was being in the right place at the right time. He would think of the right thing to do when he got there.

"Oh, Dad, that's perfect! You've got to come! Because guess who else will be here! You won't believe this. Janie. The kidnapette. She and her brother and some friend who wants to transfer are visiting Stephen. Janie's going to stay with me."

Well, well, thought Harry Donnelly. I'll encourage

the use of that word *kidnapette*. That should drive a little rift between Stephen and my daughter.

"Stephen," said Kathleen, laughing, "wanted me to promise not to ask Janie a single question. But I figure—two girls in a dorm—she has no hope. I'll know everything by morning."

And in a family so full of secrets, that should drive a second rift.

"Good idea," said her father. "Be persistent."

• • •

Janie and Reeve and Brian didn't need a single fake argument.

Everybody's parents were delighted.

Reeve's parents thought Colorado would be an excellent place to transfer to. Brian's parents had already had a thrilled call from Stephen, making them promise to pay for Brian's flight. As for Miranda Johnson, she'd actually have less to worry about with Janie away.

Janie had a worry of her own. It was twenty-four hours before the plane took off and she had not managed to be alone with her father. "I'll sit with Dad," she offered again. "Take a break, Mom. Get some fresh air."

"No, thank you, darling," said her mother. She tugged at the sheets, smoothing and neatening, as if Frank's motionless body could have disturbed anything.

Dad could breathe on his own now. His heart beat. But Dad himself, his personality and soul, was not doing much. He had yet to speak. "They"—

the shifting array of doctors and techs and nurses—
said not to give up; things could still improve.

"How about another cup of coffee, Mom?" said
Janie.

"I've had so much coffee I'm on the ceiling. I'm
excited about your trip to Colorado. Stephen is such
a fine boy. You'll have such a good rest, and think of
all that mountain air."

"Yes," said Janie. "Mom, you're so thin these
days. I want you to go down to the cafeteria and eat
something rich and filling."

Her mother said, "Actually, I have a wonderful
book on tape I'm going to play for Frank. It's the new
—"

"Mom," said Janie, pressed for time and courtesy,
"I want to say stuff to Daddy. Getting-on-a-plane
stuff. I want you to leave me alone with him for a
while."

She should have said that to start with. Her
mother lit with joy that Daddy's little girl was going
to tell him how she loved him. "Do you think he can
hear?" said her mother wistfully.

"Yes," said Janie, who was sure he could not. She
took the precaution of shutting the door when her
mother left. These weren't things she wanted Miranda to listen to.

Her father's hand was warm but limp. She could
feel its bones and see its blood vessels, but the hand
felt unoccupied. How—*how!*—could he have
screwed up so badly with the first daughter and left
the second daughter to deal with it?

I could yank out his tubes, she thought. Discon-

107

nect his monitors. I hate him, but I love him more. It isn't a rich wonderful love. I resent loving him. But it's there.

This man so flat on this mattress had no protection from the world, not even from Janie. Nothing stood between him and all things bad.

She had a sudden image of Hannah, eighteen and friendless, just this flat and unresponsive. No protection from the world. Clutching, grabbing, tightening her grip on strangers—any strangers; Hannah didn't care.

Being alone was the greatest horror plot of all time. Nobody to sit with. Nobody to phone you. Nobody to notice. Had Hannah lived inside that horror story her first eighteen years?

"I'm going to look at her, Frank," Janie said quietly. "Your real daughter. The one you put ahead of me. I'm going to see where your money and your lies went."

She waited, but there was no sign that he heard or understood or even that he was there at all. She looked down on the father who could not look back at her and began crying. "I don't know if you're in there, Daddy, or if your soul went to God and your body forgot to die. A stroke is so terrible. Everything that's happened to you is terrible, Daddy. Your very own daughter was a terrible thing to happen to you."

His monitors hummed.

"I'm going away for a few days." She felt as if she were leaving a message on his answering machine.

"Brian and I are visiting Stephen at college. Mom will be on her own."

But there was no dialogue, because there was only one speaker.

Janie turned her back on Frank Johnson.

In Colorado there would be two speakers.

There would be answers.

• • •

"How did Hannah run away that first time?" said Kathleen in the voice of one taking notes. "Did she walk? Take a bus? Train?"

"How would I know?" said Stephen. "That was years before Janie was even born. Kath, drop it. I don't want us talking about this when Janie gets here." He would have run on ahead of Kathleen, but she had twice his stamina. He had never gotten used to the thin mountain air. He couldn't pass her running up Flagstaff Mountain. A five-mile run, and Kathleen did it several times a week. It was all he could do to keep breathing at this altitude.

"You've let that kidnapette ruin your family," said Kathleen. "It is not healthy."

"Where'd you get that word? Don't call her that. She's my sister. She had to choose between two families. It was hell. It's still hell. And we are not ruined."

"Stephen, you wouldn't even admit to your own girlfriend that Janie existed. You have to let go of your anger. You have to let go of Janie."

No, thought Stephen. I have to hold on to her.

"It's important to be open," Kathleen explained.

"Yeah, well, maybe in Boulder, but in our two families it's important to leave the dark corners dark, okay?" Stephen gave up trying to pass her. He dropped back instead. He was so eager to have this visit. So glad they were coming. The last thing he wanted was Kathleen shoving Hannah Javensen into it.

Lagging behind didn't shut her up. Kathleen just slowed to his pace. "I can help, Stephen."

"Become a social worker. But leave Janie alone. Let's talk about how we're going to entertain them tomorrow."

Kathleen was scornful of people who did not use their muscles. Lazy couch potatoes needed to be taken out in the desert and made to run laps. It was her theory that Stephen's guests would want to bike up the mountains instead of seeing them from a car window.

Stephen had his doubts about that.

When at last he and Kathleen reached the mountaintop, Stephen was overwhelmed by the geography spread around him.

In New Jersey, Stephen had never known what direction he was facing. He never thought about it. But in Colorado, direction was magnificent and inescapable. East—flatness to the Mississippi. West—the Rockies. Every peak made him marvel.

He loved the West. He wanted his brother and sister and Reeve to love it too. He wanted their visit to be perfect. He was so worried that something might go wrong.

CHAPTER
THIRTEEN

Brian had flown twice, and Reeve and Janie had flown a lot. Reeve sat on the aisle, his long legs sprawled to the side. Brian had the window and was hypnotized by America thirty-five thousand feet below.

Janie sat in the middle. Reeve studied her out of the corner of his eye.

She had no book, no magazine, no crossword, no (as the flight attendant called it) electronic device. Her thoughts blazed across her face. She was a lake, her surface whipped and disturbed by thoughts of Hannah.

What if Mr. Johnson dies while we're away hunting down his other daughter? thought Reeve.

He reminded himself to make Janie call her mother every night.

He reminded himself not to do any such thing.

He napped. Nightmares leaped behind his eyelids. Hannah Javensen. Not sad and defeated, but older, meaner and more able to hurt. Hannah was a reptile, a cold-blooded thief of real children. In his dream, her skin turned snakelike and peeled away in dry scales. Her body slithered up against Janie and wrapped itself around her, a python, and yet she had the tail of a rattlesnake, and the rattles—

He woke up, his mouth dry and his neck stiff.

The rattles were Brian, flipping pages.

"Reeve, do you want the window for a while?" said Brian, leaning eagerly over Janie. His cheeks were pink and freckled, his eyes wide and excited. "It's so neat to look down on the fields, Reeve. I finally figured out that the big circles are irrigation, they're huge watering systems. For hundreds of miles, America is circles on squares."

What if they found Hannah? What if she put her hand on Brian's face or touched his hair? What if she grabbed his wrist and yanked him away with her?

● ● ●

Janie hated the middle.

She felt like a convict with prison guards. Brian to the left of her, Reeve to the right, the seat belt chaining her down.

Even eating on a plane was like prison. The warden came by with soft drinks and you were allowed one, not two. You got pretzels but couldn't order the hamburger and fries you craved.

She could not stop thinking about the Law. Law with a capital *L*, as in police and FBI and real prison.

What she needed right now was a prison library, where she could look up things like *aid and abet*. She was pretty sure that was what Frank had done when he helped Hannah leave New York. It was a crime to help a criminal. Was it less of a crime if the criminal was your daughter?

Kidnapping was a federal offense; there was no statute of limitations. Whenever Hannah was found, she would be just as guilty as she had been when she took Jennie Spring out of the shopping mall.

Was Frank just as guilty?

What would they do to him if they found out?

I'm endangering Frank, she thought.

She tightened up, trying to pull away from the observing eyes of Reeve and Brian.

And her other father, her big burly bearded father, whose greatest hope was that one day she would run toward him, laughing, and hugging, and gladder to see him than anybody.

It had not yet happened.

I could destroy both my homes doing this, Janie thought. Both my fathers. Both my mothers.

Home.

Hannah had never wanted it; Janie had wanted it so very very much.

Janie tucked her elbows in and folded her hands. She looked at the neat calm package she presented to other travelers. Travel by lying, she thought. I've stacked up lie after lie, like planes waiting to land.

I won't crash. This will work.

Sleep hit her, the kind of sleeping babies do in cars, induced by motor and vibration. In her sleep, the match that was Hannah set fire to the grass, the fire crept over the house and ate the walls, and Frank and Miranda suffocated inside.

• • •

In honor of Lewis and Clark, Brian had abandoned the Trojan War and brought the *Journals,* although Lewis and Clark had crossed the Rocky Mountains much farther north. He flipped pages but didn't read because the earth below was so fascinating. Maybe he would not study history after all. Maybe he'd become a geographer. What was there to do? Weren't all places already mapped?

The plane banked and prepared to land at Denver International Airport, and Brian saw where the Continental Divide thrust into the sky.

We got away with it, he thought. We flew across this country under false pretenses. So there, Brendan! I can do interesting stuff without you. You think *you're* the twin doing interesting things. Think again.

But *false pretenses* lay like a row of spiky nails across the road of his thoughts. What if something went wrong? What if his parents found out about this? It wasn't so much that Mom and Dad would be mad. It was that they would be crucified by having to go through it all, all over again.

The earth was rapidly getting closer and closer.

Denver International looked like a great white Arab tent in a vast and empty desert. Brian was from New Jersey. He liked buildings and people and traffic.

Once inside the terminal, however, there were enough people and traffic to go around. Everybody was rushing, dragging suitcases on squeaky wheels, shoving briefcases through crowds, glaring at monitors. Their speed infected Brian, and his excitement came back, and his delight at outwitting the world.

Stephen had instructed them to take an airport bus to Boulder. Reeve handled the details, retrieving baggage, buying their tickets, locating the right bus out of so many. Brian watched carefully, surprised to find there was nothing much to it; he could have done it. I'll handle it coming home, he told himself.

He called his parents from a pay phone to let them know he, Janie, and Reeve had landed safely, and his parents promised to call Mrs. Johnson when she got home from the hospital that night.

The Lewis and Clark book was in his way. He was almost annoyed that he'd dragged a dumb book along. They were going to be way too busy for reading. And he was going to have a million things to think about, plus evading Stephen's questions and sticking to Janie like glue, because he wasn't going to let her approach Hannah.

Lewis and Clark had no idea where they were going, Brian told himself, or how to find the West

Coast, but they got there. Janie and Reeve and I have no idea where we're going either, or how to find Hannah, but we'll get there.

The bus seats came in pairs.

Janie and Reeve sat in the row ahead of him. Brian sat alone. He stared out the window. Back East you didn't see the horizon. Trees and rooftops, dipping and rising roads, hid the sky. Rarely did you have a long view.

We don't have a long view of what we're doing, thought Brian Spring.

His excitement faded.

Fear of actually finding Hannah replaced it.

CHAPTER
FOURTEEN

No sooner had they flung their duffel bags onto the floor in Stephen's room than he insisted on a long walk to explore the campus and Boulder. Later, Stephen explained, they would meet his girlfriend, Kathleen, at their favorite sidewalk café, and close the day with a walk into the mountains.

Brian preferred cars. Actually, he preferred parking the car at the door so as to cut down on walking time. This was the way Stephen had been brought up. Now Stephen strode along like a lifelong athlete, when in fact he had been in the running for New Jersey's number one couch potato.

Brian would not give Stephen away. Nobody would know that Stephen used to spend entire weeks lying down with a remote in his hand.

He trotted at Stephen's side while Janie and Reeve followed along.

It was not possible to associate a kidnapper with this pretty bubbly active town. Everybody was out-

117

doors. This was the walkingest place Brian had ever seen. People who were not walking were running.

"It's a Colorado thing," said Stephen. "People are into running."

"Are you running now?" asked Brian respectfully.

"Kathleen runs," said Stephen. "Sometimes I trot along. I'm getting to be pretty decent on a bike."

"I would only do the part where you coast," said Brian.

Just a few blocks of houses stood between them and the start of the Rocky Mountains. The foothills were right there. Brian was awestruck.

"It's called the Front Range," said Stephen. "I love that. I'm in front. I'm on the range."

There were tiny brick parks and a fountain; benches and a juggler and a chalk artist. There were enough street musicians that everybody's music blended into everybody else's, and the din was like the races, only tuneful.

They turned a corner and across the street was the Boulder post office.

Brian's knees stiffened and his mouth gave a funny jerk, as if he had bitten down on a lemon. The woman who had mutilated their lives must walk in and out of those doors. Her fingers must hold those handles and her eyes stare out of that glass. In that building was the box where she got her money.

The sunny laughing warmth of Boulder was unchanged, but Brian stood in the shade. It was real. Janie really meant to do this.

"Bri?" said Stephen. "You okay?"

"Oh, yeah, sure," said Brian. "Well, maybe I'm hungry."

"Planes are terrible," said Stephen sympathetically. "They never give you anything but pretzels. We'll head to the café right now."

Brian had never encountered a sympathic Stephen. Suffer and shut up about it, was Stephen's theory.

"What do you feel like having, Bri?" said Stephen in a comforting voice Brian did not remember. "Real food, ice cream, just a Coke or what?"

I want to go home, thought Brian. I want us not to be doing this. I want not to find Hannah.

• • •

Reeve walked a little behind the three Springs.

He loved exercise and had gotten extra used to it this summer because he had no car, but he found walking through Boulder deeply upsetting. What if that middle-aged woman walking a dog, or that one on a bike, or that one window-shopping was Hannah?

There was something dreadful about the brightness of light in the West. Nothing could be hidden from that sun.

He stared at Stephen's back and thought, I can't stop Janie. But *you* could. Do I tell you?

Lord, if only I could tell up front when I'm being a jerk.

• • •

119

"Boulder is charming," said Janie. "I like it here, Stephen. I've never been in such a people town. I love all the little shops and sidewalk cafés. I want to live here and go in each one and eat all day, except for when I'm shopping."

Shopping was the last thing on Janie's mind. When they walked past the post office, her heart shot forward, leaped inside and stood in front of tiny boxes with tiny keyholes. If I could ask Hannah Javensen just one question, thought Janie, only one—what would it be?

"It is a neat town," agreed Stephen.

Janie despised liars, and here she stood, blithely lying with her smile, her posture, her voice and her topics. She glanced around for another lying topic to hide behind.

Even the clothing here was different. At home, everybody would be wearing sneakers. Here, just as many people wore sandals. She had never seen grown women wearing cowboy boots. "I want cowboy boots," said Janie, and that particular lie became truth, because right away she really did want cowboy boots.

"We are not here to shop," said Brian firmly.

"But if we were," said Stephen, "we could easily find the right boots." He steered them toward a gathering of round white tables with stools tilting around like little hungry people.

If I had one question, she thought, I would ask, *Who failed?* Did you fail our parents, Hannah? Or did they fail you?

My wonderful parents who did everything right and loved me so. Were they crummy parents to you? What was your childhood? Was it the same as mine? Did they really love you? Did they do their best?

Then why did you turn out bad?

"Kathleen's father says Boulder is dreamland," said Stephen. "This is a town for people who don't have both feet on the ground. Like—for example— look at that guy in the torn shorts."

The man was fortyish. His hair long and loose, he was running barefoot, singing along to the music on his earphones. He looked as if he might have bathed last week, or then again, he might have skipped it.

"Boulder is full of people who don't work," said Stephen, marveling. "Or they work now and then. Or if the spirit moves them. Meanwhile they soak up mountain air and the aura of the earth. And guess who pays the bills?" Stephen shook his head. "Their parents. Can you believe that? After all these years? These guys run up the mountains and down the creek path and then they run to the post office and get their little monthly checks."

Janie believed it.

• • •

Stephen flagged a waiter. Then he smiled a smile as happy as Brian had ever seen on his brother's face. "Here comes Kathleen," said Stephen. "She said she'd find us."

So Stephen was not just in love with the West. He

121

was in love with a girl. Brian checked Kathleen out thoroughly. She was long and lean and very tan. She wore no makeup, no socks and no jewelry.

"Hey, you guys! I knew you from a block away!" She enclosed Janie's two cheeks in her hands, air-kissed each one and said, "I'm Kathleen. I'm so glad to meet you. You've got Stephen's hair. Of course, he cuts his off. He should let it grow. Don't you think he'd be adorable in a ponytail?"

Brian did not think Stephen could be adorable under any circumstance or hairstyle. Stephen was shaped like a tire iron, all his bones a little too long: too long in the forehead, too long in the neck, too long in the waist. His clothing fell around him as if any minute it would just leave and he'd be un-dressed in the street.

How nice that a beautiful girl thought Stephen was adorable.

Kathleen stroked Brian's entire head with her palms. "Yours is nice too, but half an inch isn't enough, Brian. People like you add color to the world. It's your duty to let your hair grow." She said, "Stephen, what are you ordering? Did you order enough to share?" She said, "Waiter! We need you again!" She said, "So you're Reeve! Well? Are you transferring here? What's your major? I wonder if we'll have classes together." She said, "Welcome to Boulder, everybody."

Brian loved her. He took a long thick straw-suck of his chocolate milk shake and didn't even mind when Kathleen said he must try wheatgrass. They sat around on the hard little stools and Stephen looked happy. He even looked soft. Maybe even relaxed.

Kathleen took a huge bite of a veggie pita sandwich from which bean sprouts hung like lace. "You need to know, Janie, that Stephen told me the basic outlines. But he left out the details, and he doesn't want me to ask a thing because your family is into dark corners, but I have about six hundred questions waiting."

Janie did not tackle the six hundred questions. "What I want to talk about," she said, "is where to buy cowboy boots."

"Ahh, a shopper," said Kathleen. "You've come to the right town. Boots are expensive, though, did you bring lots of money or a credit card? You don't want cheap ones, and the purchase of cowboy boots will not deflect me from my questions." She gave Janie a dazzling smile and Brian did not like her after all. Kathleen expected to get her way with that smile, and probably always did. Brian studied the bottom of his milk shake and stirred chocolate bubbles.

"I was hoping, Janie," said Kathleen with a smile so wide it was almost a glare, "that we'd stay awake all night, a two-girl slumber party, and you'd tell me everything."

Brian could not look at his sister or his brother. They had been here, done this. People were so drawn to Janie's history. You could slap them in the face with how much you didn't want to talk about it, and still they would not let go.

"Cut it out, Kathleen," said Stephen.

Kathleen ignored him. "I cannot wait to get your

viewpoint on Hannah Javensen," she said to Janie. "Why did she do it? Why you?"

• • •

Janie drank a lot of Coke fast. The familiar icy shock helped. Reeve's hand landed in hers, his fingers taking hold, and the closeness of their hands felt good. He was hot. Not the hot of slang, meaning desirable, but the hot of temperature. Reeve's physical warmth always startled her, and now the smooth kindness of his skin against hers overwhelmed her. She remembered, suddenly, how much she had loved him.

"Janie?" said Stephen. "You okay?"

"I got sideswiped when Kathleen said Hannah Javensen's name," she admitted. "You'd think it wouldn't mean a thing by now."

Stephen shrugged. "I still have daydreams where I throw the kidnapper over a cliff and watch her bounce off rocks and get impaled a thousand feet below."

Reeve's grip tightened on Janie's hand.

Brian chewed on a curly french fry. After a while, he said, "Suppose she showed up, Stephen? What would you do?"

"I'd have her in jail in a heartbeat," he said. "Of course, it would be my heart beating, because Hannah Javensen never had a heart. But ten seconds after I figured out who she was, she'd be locked up."

The sun burned their faces.

"I think," said Reeve, "that I am going to have a hamburger after all. I am starved. Stephen, how do meals work on this campus? When you're a student. You have a dining room or what? Because in Boston, you don't sign up for the dining room if you don't want. There's so much takeout. Or vendors, delis, whatever."

Stephen and Kathleen had a lot to say about food, and the anger in Stephen's voice slid slowly away.

● ● ●

They wandered up and down the shopping streets of Boulder. Stephen and Kathleen held hands. Reeve, uncertain, took Janie's once more. She squeezed his and he thought, Whoa. Not bad.

"It's just a hand," she said to him.

"It's probably five percent of my body, though," said Reeve, "five percent with lots of nerve endings and hope." Then he almost snapped her wrist, jerking forward, calling sharply, "Brian! Stay with me."

Kathleen turned, incredulous, to look at Reeve.

"Sorry," muttered Reeve. He gave Brian an embarrassed wave and could not meet Stephen's eyes. He thought, I can't stand this. I can't watch some sidewalk vendor twist balloons into animal shapes while I'm thinking, *Hannah walks here.*

"Look," said Janie brightly, "a pawnshop. I've never been in one."

"Mom would not give us permission to go in," said Brian.

Kathleen giggled.

"Stephen, you're the oldest," said Janie. "Give us permission to go in a pawnshop."

"It's just a store, I think. I've never been in one

either. All it does is sell stuff people want to get rid of."

"Boots!" shrieked Janie. "Look in the window! On that shelf! Beautiful red perfect gorgeous cowboy boots. I didn't know leather came in red. Are they leather, do you think, Kathleen? They're girls' boots, aren't they?"

Kathleen said, "Brian, may we please have permission to enter this building and investigate those boots?"

"You've never asked permission in your life," said Brian, staring at Kathleen.

"No, but I've heard about your permissions. You guys cannot enter danger zones unless you hold hands." Kathleen burst out laughing and flung open the door to the pawnshop.

If Stephen stays with her, thought Brian, she'll never quite get it right. She'll always think it's a little bit funny, when it's always a little bit nightmarish. But maybe that's okay. Maybe Stephen needs somebody to poke fun at it.

His brother was right. The pawnshop was just a secondhand store.

The clerk got the red boots down. "Size six," he said. "Very high quality. Some college girl bought 'em the first week she was here, ran out of money and hocked 'em. Lots of people been in and want 'em, but nobody fits 'em."

Janie unlaced her sneakers and slid her small feet in their plain white socks into the boots. "They fit!" She danced down the aisle.

The boots were wonderful, but they were also nothing. They were a diversion. She was going to need a lot of diversions. Because it was not just Brian and Reeve she had to get rid of. It was also the very pushy Kathleen and the very observant Stephen.

All Brian had had to do was get half a block ahead of them, and Reeve had panicked. As for Brian, one glimpse of the post office and *he* had panicked. A few more episodes like that, and Stephen would start asking questions.

When the clerk said how much the boots cost—even secondhand! even here!—Janie's face fell. If she spent that much on boots, she wouldn't be able to afford the bus back to the airport.

"You know what, Janie?" said Stephen. "I've never gotten you a present." His smile was truly sweet; this older brother who had despised her last year. "I'm buying you those."

All those birthdays, she thought. All those Christmases. Without presents between us. Hannah took away every Christmas morning, every Christmas carol, every Christmas present.

Their eyes met, hers and Stephen's, and she thought: Stephen and I are the closest of all. Reeve walked beside me when this unfolded, and he knows most of it, but it isn't his. Brian was too young and too twinned to be inside the whole of it. Kathleen is a stranger. But Stephen and I, we possess our history together. We're both still so angry.

Stephen paid for the boots with ones. How he enjoyed counting out those bills he had earned one sweaty dollar at a time. The price was a stretch for him. Maybe a sacrifice.

And I, thought Janie, am not about to sacrifice anything for anybody. I have my questions. I'm going to ask them.

● ● ●

Reeve and Brian were sleeping on the floor in Stephen's room, in borrowed sleeping bags.

Kathleen had no roommate for the summer, so she spread her sleeping bag on the bare mattress of the empty second bed for Janie. It felt oddly intimate to use somebody else's sleeping bag.

"That might be too hot," said Kathleen.

"Oh, no, it's perfect. I always sleep like a rock. I'm usually asleep within twenty seconds."

"Yeah, right," said Kathleen. "You just don't want to be a decent guest and talk all night."

Janie said nothing.

"You want to go out with me for a run in the morning?" asked Kathleen. "I take off about six when it's still cool and head into the mountains."

"I can't run up those hills. Can you stand to run in the town part of Boulder? On sidewalks? Like, say, going past the library and the post office?"

It was not precisely another lie. But it would have the result of a lie. Inside the hot sleeping bag, Janie shivered, and wondered if H. J. would see her froth of red hair, and remember.

CHAPTER
FIFTEEN

Six A.M. was just as early and horrible as it sounded and Kathleen's alarm clock could have been mistaken for a chain saw.

"My approach," said Kathleen, vaulting off her mattress to begin stretching exercises, "is to be firm with myself at all times. Slack off and weakness sets in."

Fly two thousand miles, and you meet yet another perfectionist. Janie moaned and peeled down her sleeping bag. How could Kathleen have softened Stephen?

It seemed best not to look in a mirror but just to yank on clothes and stagger out, hoping not to fall down the stairs.

Kathleen ran like a rabbit while Janie tottered like an old breathless dog. Kathleen said things like "So do you really believe your Johnson parents didn't know you were kidnapped?" and Janie said things like "What is that building over there, with the tower?"

When they were within sight of the post office, Janie said, "I am whipped! Kathleen, you are too much for me. What an athlete you are! I'll just rest here. On that bench. I can find my way back to the dorm."

"Great!" said Kathleen, already half a block away.

Lying to Kathleen was fun. It didn't count, the way lying to Stephen and Reeve and Brian did.

Even at this hour, Boulder was active.

Two women, walking fast and talking faster, strode toward Janie. They had weights strapped to their ankles and were carrying weights in their hands. Their age was hard to guess. Fit and tan, they could have been anything from thirty to fifty.

But Janie could not imagine Hannah having friends. They weren't Hannah.

And then, in sneakers so padded she made no sound whatsoever, a woman came up from behind and sat next to Janie on the bench. Right next to her. Almost hip to hip. Janie knew it was a woman from the legs, but she could not bring herself to look at the face.

What if it was Hannah? Would there be a flicker of Miranda Johnson, a hint of Frank, in the woman's eyes?

Janie wiped sweaty palms on her khaki shorts. She focused on the post office across from her and tried to plan her attack. The five tall and shining numbers on the post office exterior were not the zip code written on the file folder.

Terrific. Boulder had more than one post office.

That doesn't matter, Janie told herself. I'm not going to watch her pick up her letter anyway. We're going to meet in some other place.

The check was now late.

If you received income four times a year, you would be feeling desperate now, wouldn't you? You'd be hanging out at the post office, waiting, wouldn't you?

She'll be there first thing Monday morning, thought Janie, because I bet she doesn't have a job to go to. Just a box to check.

The problem isn't Hannah. *She'll* come. The problem is everybody else. *They'll* come. I have to get away from them.

I have to decide right now where Hannah is going to meet me. And how I'll describe myself. I won't tell her who I am, that would scare her off. I'll say I'm a messenger from Frank Johnson. I'll say, Look for red hair.

Janie got up carefully, keeping her head stiffly tilted so she could not see the woman on the bench, and walked back to Kathleen's dorm.

• • •

It was decided that they would bicycle up Flagstaff Mountain.

Brian was not in on the decision. But he was determined to go along and not whimper. If he gave up, he'd get left out of everything.

The trip was more ghastly than Brian could have imagined. Many times more ghastly. It turned out that mountains had beauty and mountains had fabulous views. Mountains did not have air. There really was such a thing as thin mountain air. Brian could not satisfy his lungs on such low-calorie air. And then—to bike uphill?

Forget whimpering. Focus on not dying.

Kathleen didn't stop asking questions, but Janie was puffing even more than Brian and had no air for speech. When they weren't gasping for breath, Reeve and Janie and Brian were laughing at themselves. Nobody had pictured the trip to Boulder like this.

"I give up," moaned Janie. "I'm a weakling."

"Yay," whispered Brian, summoning the energy to clap once.

Much to Kathleen's dismay, they turned around and coasted home so that the jet-lagged people could nap.

• • •

Waking up from a nap is not the same as waking up from a night.

Nap sleep takes hold; is heavy and deep.

The fingers that closed on Janie's bare arm pressed down with long hard nails. The hand tightened, and shook her, and shoved slightly, as if to dislocate the shoulder. Janie woke up as if she were being attacked; torn from safety, thrown into danger.

She woke as if she were being kidnapped, heart thrashing, soul coming loose.

"Time to go, Janie, time to go!" cried Kathleen.

She sounded like a crow over a field. Again she shook Janie, hard; her fingers weirdly possessive.

When I was kidnapped, a hand owned me like that, thought Janie. A woman's fingers caught my arm, right there, and hauled me away, like this.

This is how my New Jersey mother woke up in the night, thought Janie. Feeling my kidnapping in her heart. Feeling the hand that held me. Year in, year out, feeling the fingers that grabbed me.

How forcefully Janie understood then that Hannah Javensen had no excuse. Not the slightest fraction of an excuse. There would never be an excuse for ripping a child from her family.

"I let you sleep as long as I could, Jennie-Janie," said Kathleen. "Now get up! We're going to car races at the Rocky Mountain National Speedway. Stephen got tickets in honor of Reeve."

"Right," said Janie, thinking, I can't lose my temper, Stephen loves her. She swung off the bed, damp with the sweat of heavy sleep, and struggled down the hall to the bathroom.

Kathleen came right after her. "I've never been to a car race. Is it fun?"

Janie's mouth was so dry she drank from the faucet in one of the sinks. She splashed water on her face and throat and didn't dry it off.

I was kidnapped. My parents are not my parents. I threw away my real parents to keep the parents who were not my parents. But they didn't throw away their real daughter. They kept her first, they kept me second.

They kept me.

133

It's all about keeping.

Who keeps who?

Does a good Frank keep an evil Hannah? Does a good Janie . . . ?

Or am I ready to be a bad Janie?

"Reeve said to wear old crummy clothes," said Kathleen. She threw her huge smile at Janie and big white teeth gleamed in a dozen mirrors.

"You're going to get filthy," agreed Janie. She crossed the tiny white and gray and black tiles and closed herself inside one of the stalls.

"What are the races like?" demanded Kathleen.

"You're going to go deaf. You're going to eat the worst tacos in the entire nation."

"Hey, cool," said Kathleen. "I can't wait." And she didn't wait. She began pacing the tile floors.

If I look down at the toilet, thought Janie, I'll throw up in it.

Keeping her back to the toilet, she pressed her forehead against the gray metal enclosure, and suddenly under the door appeared the tips of Kathleen's open-toed sandals, pressing against her own bare feet.

"What are you doing in there?" said Kathleen crossly.

Reviewing my life, thought Janie. Considering homicide.

"Reeve says you love races," said Kathleen.

"You get great jewelry," Janie said to the toes. "Paper bracelets with racing flags." She lifted her eyes and stared ahead so that she no longer saw

Kathleen's toes but was looking straight into the steel gray door.

This is what you deserve, Hannah, thought Janie. A view of steel doors.

And is that what I should be arranging instead of gazing stupidly at post office windows?

Steel doors for Hannah?

• • •

Kathleen borrowed a friend's car and drove them to the racetrack. It was a long haul, and even though Denver was right there, the track itself seemed to be in the middle of a wilderness.

Once they were settled in the stands, Janie positioned her purse between her feet. She normally carried a tiny purse or none at all, but for the trip, to hold tickets, paperbacks, hand lotion, hairbrush, a camera and the H. J. checkbook, she had acquired a roomy satchel. She wasn't used to it and felt a constant obligation to check. Did she still have it, were the plane tickets still there, was the checkbook?

She tucked her sandals up close, curving her ankles until she could feel the purse against her skin. Everybody else is here to watch cars go in circles, she thought. I'm here to stop running in circles. I've circled enough. It's time to close in.

"That," said Stephen, pointing to the wilderness around them, "is the Rocky Mountain Arsenal. See the high chain-link fence and the barbed wire? They used to practice chemical warfare here, but now

135

they're cleaning up. Every now and then you see MPs patrolling in Jeeps to make sure nobody trespasses. If your feet touch the ground, poison seeps through your shoes."

"Really?" said Brian, thrilled. He jumped up and shaded his eyes, hoping to see MPs capturing hikers. To Janie he whispered, "I have to get to a library or an Internet site and find out if that's true."

The first cars came out onto the track. Reeve discussed racing rules. Stephen said he'd forgotten his sunglasses. Kathleen said, "If only we had a camera."

Janie opened her mouth to say, We do, I brought a disposable camera.

But she did not want to open the purse in front of anybody. She had zipped her plans inside there, and the camera was for taking a photo of Hannah. Although she was not sure what she planned to do with a shot of Hannah. Give it to Frank? Tape it on the refrigerator? She imagined herself telling her kidnapper to pose. Get the light right. Smile.

The first race began. Kathleen gasped and covered her ears. The boys leaned forward, discussing strategy.

On Monday, both Stephen and Kathleen had to work; Janie and Brian and Reeve, they said sadly, would have to manage without them.

The problem, thought Janie, is making Brian and Reeve manage without *me*. How do I dump them? Should I set up a college interview and go by myself? Or get silly and Hollywoody, slip through buildings when the boys aren't looking, go out the back, leave them waiting for hours in a lobby?

No, the easiest thing would be to claim exhaustion and return alone to Kathleen's room for a nap.

I'll tell the boys I've given up the idea of staking out the post office, she decided. I'll tell Reeve he was absolutely right, I'm just mailing the check, anything more is too creepy. None of us will go look for Hannah.

Adding one more lie to the manure pile of lies that ruled her life made Janie duck beneath her hair. But there was so much sun on this prairie. Such bright light! There was no place to hide.

How had her father kept so many secrets for so long? It must have eaten into his gut like cancer.

No, she remembered.

Into his heart.

When the race ended, Stephen turned happily to Kathleen to see if she had enjoyed it, and Janie thought: I've got to photograph that for Mom, Stephen smiling and soft in his new world.

It was her New Jersey mother she meant.

She felt like a person in a cartoon, straddling cracks in the earth where quakes had torn apart the land. She had to keep a foot in New Jersey, a foot in Connecticut, a foot in Colorado, a foot in revenge, a foot in—

But nobody could do that. You fell through the cracks instead.

"Isn't the Arsenal a little close to the taco stand?" said Reeve. "If there *is* poison leaching—"

137

"Eastern wimps worry about this stuff," said Stephen. "We Westerners, we're tough. We shrug. We're real men."

It turned out that real men didn't use the cement-block bathrooms, either. They walked up to the fence and peed through the chain links, joking about fumes that would suffocate fellow racers. There seemed no end to the stupid jokes Reeve and Stephen could make about this.

Boys being friends always attracted Janie. Their friendships were so different from girls' friendships. Now she was just glad their minds were occupied.

She planned what to write in her letter to Hannah. She unzipped the purse just wide enough to thrust her hand in and make sure her writing supplies were there. On top lay her cell phone.

Back home, Janie called her mother constantly. She called if she was next door, or at Sarah-Charlotte's, or at school. Now she was two thousand miles away and not calling.

Distance was so real. You could feel it.

All two thousand miles stood fat and sturdy between Janie and that hospital bed. From this distance, the man and woman in that room were dots, not people. You didn't have to worry about dots.

• • •

Stephen said, "Come on, Bri, let's you and me hike around, see what there is to eat."

When they were behind the stands and the roar of cars had diminished, Stephen said abruptly, "Tell me about your worthless twin. Is he still being a jerk?"

"He's not worthless. He's an incredible athlete, Stephen. He—"

"He's worthless," said Stephen. "Last week on the phone I talked to Mom and then Dad and then Jodie. They had to force Brendan onto the phone. He tells me, this jerk starting ninth grade in September, that he's already chosen his college. Duke. He says he isn't smart enough to get in, but as long as *you* write his papers for him he'll be okay. Have you been doing that, Brian? Admit it. Are you cheating for him?"

Brian was helpless. "He's my twin."

"Brian, I'm telling Mom and Dad—"

"No!"

"—to put you in a different school. There's a Catholic boys' school, it's very academic, just right for you, and you'd be away from your worthless twin."

"You would have taken a garbage route before you'd have gone to Xavier, Stephen," said Brian. "And don't call him worthless, he's your brother."

"Many brothers are worthless," said Stephen. "Yup. This is the solution. It'll untwin you. Brendan already untwinned, the skunk, and it's time you did the same."

Brian nodded, although he would never untwin; he couldn't have if he'd wanted to; birth bound him too tightly.

"Bri, lighten up," said his brother. "Is it Bren you're upset about? Janie? Reeve? Reeve with Janie?"

139

Brian imagined the kidnapper contaminating Janie or Stephen, as the Arsenal was contaminated.

"You're acting like I'm a threat," said his brother. "What's going on?"

Brian's head swam with unfamilies. Hannah had been an undaughter. Stephen wanted Brian to untwin.

"I guess I got too close to Janie's other family," he said at last. "I'm worried about Mr. Johnson dying or being a vegetable. I'm worried about Mrs. Johnson being by herself and I'm worried about Janie making stupid decisions."

"Like what?" said Stephen, who had never been slow. "What stupid decision does she have in mind right now?"

• • •

Reeve was not surprised when Kathleen jumped up after five minutes and said she thought she'd go find Stephen.

Girls who want you for themselves, he thought, even when you go off with a kid brother you haven't seen in months—they're trouble.

He turned to share his thoughts with Janie and got her hair in his face. Today it was the approximate size and shape of a bushel of apples. How he wanted to run his fingers through the mass of her hair.

She had opened her purse and was digging around in it. It would have made Reeve crazy to carry that thing around.

She pulled out the checkbook.

The hot sun suddenly blistered him. He did not want her writing Hannah Johnson's name, with her own fingers curled around her own pen. Hannah Johnson didn't even exist! She was a falsehood. There was only Hannah Javensen, kidnapper.

But in Janie's life, H. J. was a force stronger than gravity.

Reeve felt frantic and yet heavy; his thoughts impossible to pin down, his body too thick to respond.

He had agreed to this! He had even suggested the format for coming.

"Janie, forget it," he said. "Let Hannah float downstream without you. Grown-ups have to take care of themselves. Cut her off."

He himself might once have cut Hannah off.

Reeve had gotten involved in his college radio station, narrating a soap opera: a nightly episode of Janie. The kidnapping, the milk carton, the courts, the birth family, all audience-pleasers. He'd blatted about Janie's tears and failure of spirit. It entertained his listeners just fine until one night his listeners included Janie.

Trust and love were dead in minutes.

But what Janie didn't know—nobody else knew—was that a phone call had been made to the station late one night. When he picked up, Reeve expected the usual band request, but the caller said she was Janie Johnson's kidnapper. Without thinking—a frequent problem for Reeve—he disconnected. Stupid move, because the woman didn't call back.

One or two questions, and he'd have known whether it was Hannah from a pay phone or a silly college kid hoping for airtime.

A thousand times he had wondered: Am I the only one who ever actually spoke to the kidnapper?

That would have placed her in Boston last fall, and not in Colorado.

But she had enough money from Frank to get on a bus and visit friends. If you could imagine Hannah having friends. Ex–cult members, maybe. Reeve didn't think Hannah would go to Boston to see Paul Revere's house.

Reeve hadn't done the right thing once in his entire freshman year. The only good things about his eighteenth year were the things he hadn't done: He hadn't murdered anybody or sold drugs.

I have to do the right thing this time, Reeve told himself. And what might that be?

The super stocks went round and round, mud covering the names of their sponsors.

"I'm scared for you, Janie," said Reeve.

Janie watched the race. "She's not going to attack me."

"Janie, no matter how sweetly you remember it, with the ice cream and the twirling stool and skipping along the sidewalks, kidnapping is a violent crime."

But they were out of time for private conversation and she wasn't listening to him anyway. The others were returning, Brian walking by himself, kicking at clods of dirt thrown up by the race cars. Kathleen had Stephen by the hand.

They were coming up the bleachers as Janie wrote the check, capped her ball pen and dropped pen and checkbook back into her purse.

The check horrified him. Her casual attitude horrified him.

And then Reeve figured it out. The check didn't matter because she was going to talk to Hannah. All that mattered to Janie Johnson right now were her questions and her answers. The check was just a way to get hold of Hannah.

He threw it all away, every minute and every month of trying to win Janie back. He said fiercely, "Janie. *Stop it.* You find Hannah, and you're betraying your father and mother as badly as I betrayed you."

• • •

How dare you? thought Janie. How dare you compare your nasty little radio trick with what I am facing? I am not betraying my father. He betrayed me! And I deserve answers.

Stephen sat down next to her, with Brian on his other side, so that Kathleen was left to sit wherever. Kathleen did not like this. Stephen did not appear to notice. "What's the stupid decision Brian was telling me about?" he said, smiling at Janie.

Stephen's eyes were their mother's eyes. Her New Jersey mother. Her real mother, who would be so disappointed in her right now. Make us proud, they had said to Janie when she left them for good.

"I didn't tell him anything," said Brian quickly. He jerked his head toward Kathleen, saying as plainly

143

as words that she had shown up and ended their talk.

Janie thought of a way to deflect Stephen that was not actually a lie.

"There was this file in my father's desk," she told Stephen. "Old papers. The police report on Hannah Javensen and stuff."

She could feel Brian's fear that she was going to tell everything. She hoped he held together.

"There was this sentence in the police report," she said to Stephen. "*The subject was last seen flying west.* That sentence crawls around under my skin like a tropical disease. I love the idea of being last seen. Ditching the whole thing. Disappearing. Think about it, Stephen. You disappear, you have the power of a god. If you vanish, you control your family forever."

Reeve tilted away from her, his spine stiff as a chair, his big warm features growing long and thin with surprise and distaste. Good. She felt the same toward him.

"*You're* not the one who has to be the good guy, Stephen," Janie said. "*I'm* the one. You guys thought I was the bad guy when I left New Jersey and went home, but I was just being the good guy for my other family. And when Reeve was a jerk last year, I was supposed to be the good guy again. And when my father got sick, I *really* had to be the good guy. And my stupid decision is: I'm sick of being the good guy. I could be last seen flying west too, you know."

Brian looked ill.

Reeve looked away.

Kathleen was mesmerized.

Stephen just grinned. "I totally understand. I was last seen flying west, Janie, and I'm not going east again. I made sure nobody else was kidnapped. I did dishes, I mowed the lawn, I washed the car, I finished my homework. If I had to swear at my teachers, I did it under my breath. That's all the good guy I'm going to be."

And that's all the truth I'm going to tell, thought Janie. Because on Monday, I will be the bad guy. I will meet Hannah.

She made a topknot of her hair and swished her forehead with it.

"You already vanished from our lives twice, Janie," said Stephen. "You can't do it again. Got to stomp on that one. What you can do is work around the edges. Distance is good. You like it in Colorado? Come here next year. Your parents would go for it."

Distance was good. It was easy to do what you wanted when you didn't have to show up for dinner with the people you were hurting.

"But what did Reeve do to be a jerk?" said Kathleen, tugging at Stephen's shirt. "Tell me, I love stories like that."

Reeve gazed at the Arsenal, obviously picking a spot for Kathleen to soak up poison.

"Beats me," said Stephen. "When Reeve came to New Jersey at first everyone loved him. He made things easier. But then nobody talked about Reeve anymore. Mom made a face every time his name came up. Janie wasn't going out with him, and when I mentioned him, Jodie stuck her finger down her throat and gagged. So my wild guess was that we hated him." Stephen laughed. "I'm a good hater, I joined up." He smiled and said gently to his sister, "But I liked Reeve, so when you were seeing him again, it was fine with me. I unhated."

Janie let go of her hair, shaking herself to free the curls.

Kathleen leaned around the three Springs. "What *did* you do, Reeve?" she asked with her silken smile.

CHAPTER
SIXTEEN

They left the races early.

The girls headed for Kathleen's room to scrub off track grime and get into something nice for dinner. While Kathleen was blowing her hair dry—something Janie could never do or she would have a red pyramid for a head—Janie said, "I have to mail a letter. I'm just going to run over to that box by the student center. I'll meet you at Stephen's dorm."

"I might take a few minutes," said Kathleen. "I have to change the reservations. Make sure the boys look decent, Janie. We're not just getting pizza."

As if I don't have enough to worry about without enforcing dress codes, thought Janie.

She walked out of Kathleen's room, shut the door carefully and, instead of going to the stairs, followed the corridor until she arrived in the dorm commons: a sunny bright place with a television, a few

Internet-dedicated computers, two sofas and some vending machines.

Nobody was there.

In summer, the dorm had a hot, waiting feel: dust collecting and thoughts set down.

Janie sat at one of the small slanting desks, designed before laptops needing flat low surfaces; designed for three-ring binders and sharp pencils. She opened her purse.

There was the envelope, stamped and addressed. There were three sheets of plain white writing paper, in case she made mistakes and had to make a second or even a third try at the letter to Hannah.

She took out the ballpoint pen and uncapped it.

Her hands got cold. She put the pen back and took out a pencil instead. She felt safer in pencil.

DEAR HANNAH, she wrote, and the words leaped off the page and screamed at her. There was nothing "dear" about Hannah.

This is not a letter, Janie reminded herself. This is a set of instructions. I'm going to tell her where and when. I'm going to leave out who and why. We'll get to that when we talk.

She folded down an inch of paper, creased it with her fingernail and tore away the DEAR HANNAH.

She quit using block letters. It felt criminal, as if Janie were demanding a ransom.

> *Frank Johnson has asked me to deliver*
> *your check by hand. He needs to know if*
> *he is giving you enough money, or if you*
> *need more.*

That idea had come to her in the night and it was brilliant. How could Hannah resist more money?

> *Meet me in the university library magazine room.*

What could be safer?

Libraries were full of people browsing here and there. She and Hannah would blend. But what time Monday? If Hannah did have a job, she wouldn't be free until five or six. But by five or six, Stephen would be back from work, the boys would be hungry and Kathleen would be pouncing on everybody like a fox after mice.

It's money, Janie told herself. Hannah never ignored the money before. She won't ignore it now. She'll get out of work to get the money.

At one-thirty, Janie would claim jet lag and leave Brian and Reeve and go to Kathleen's room. Reeve would trust Janie to do what she said.

She wrote:

> *Two p.m.*

Her hand shook. The writing was barely legible.

Her hand was so damp with perspiration, it left a complete and perfect five-fingered print on the paper. She would have to copy the letter over and use this effort as a blotter so that she didn't pawprint again.

How was Hannah to know which person in the magazine room?

Janie's identifying mark was certainly her bushel of red hair. But did she really want to refer to her hair, age and looks? Once they started talking, it would become clear that she was the tiny child Hannah had snatched all those years ago. But Janie needed to build up to that, or Hannah might take flight.

It's a magazine room, she reminded herself. The signal can just be a magazine. She wrote:

I will be reading National Geographic.

Janie copied the note, folded it, put it in the envelope and sealed it. She went down the stairs farthest from Kathleen's side of the dorm and out the back, following paths over the grass, passing under trees and around shrubbery to a fat blue curved mailbox.

It was Saturday, seven P.M. Mail, the placard on the box said, would be retrieved Sunday at eight A.M.

The lid was protected by a blue overhang. Dropping her purse on the ground, Janie took the mailbox handle in her right hand and opened the slot.

Her left hand clutched convulsively on the envelope, wrinkling it badly. She had to stand for a moment, hanging on to the blue box, until a sick dizziness passed.

Do it, she said to herself. Don't wimp out now. You came here to do this. Do it.

● ● ●

The boys took very hot showers, soaking out filth and grit and letting their muscles relax. When he was clean and had shaved, Stephen put on shorts and a T-shirt, so Brian and Reeve did too. The best thing about college was that you could wear anything anywhere.

"Kath picked a place for dinner," said Stephen. "I'd rather order pizza, but she likes restaurants."

"How can you afford all this?" said Brian.

"Actually, I'm not sure how I'm going to afford tonight. I may have to veto her restaurant choice."

"I have money," said Reeve. "If it isn't too expensive, I can pay."

They counted the available cash and suddenly they were starving, desperate, in pain, not a single interest in life except food and lots of it. They charged down the stairs and burst out the front door to meet the girls.

The campus road was quiet.

There was no traffic, there were no other people.

The shadows were long and dark.

The sky was thick and sullen, the color of suffocation.

Janie appeared in the distance, coming alone down a narrow path. She wore a long thin cotton dress that caught at her ankles. It was white, with tiny embroidered white flowers. Just washed, her hair was beginning to dry, and each separate curl was sproinging up.

She was so vivid; so noticeable.

The degree to which she stood out was frightening.

She stood out like that when she was three, thought Stephen. That's why Hannah Javensen wanted her. She was an adorable doll to pick up and carry along.

Stephen felt queerly responsible, as if something were about to happen; as if, like a bird before a storm, he could feel a change in the weather. A change for the worse.

Janie had a strange expression on her face, like a toddler who knows she has done something wrong; who expects punishment.

Slowly, down the campus road, came a single car, its engine so well designed it was nearly silent. It was a black Lincoln Town Car, heavy doors and shadowed glass.

They all turned to watch it, Stephen with his undefined anxiety; Reeve with his nerves shot; Brian hungry; Janie walking as if she would like to be someplace else.

The car stopped in front of the boys while Janie was still several feet away. Stephen recognized the driver and felt his visit crumbling. This, then, must be the punishment Janie was expecting: yet another interrogation.

"What are you doing here?" Stephen demanded. He walked sideways, not taking his eyes off the Lincoln, to stand in front of Janie. He knew he was not thinking clearly. He could not reach clarity. He said, "Get out of here."

Kathleen opened the passenger's door. "Stephen,"

she said, astonished. "What's the matter with you? Dad just happened to be in town again. He's taking us all to dinner."

"FBI agents don't just happen to be places," said Stephen. "Get away from us. My sister isn't talking to you."

Harry Donnelly got out of the car too, standing in the L of the open driver's door. He held up his two hands for peace. "Stephen, I'm just here as Kathleen's dad. I'm really not thinking of anything but a good meal and some good conversation."

"Think again!" Stephen could not stand it. Literally. He felt that his body might take wing, or swim, because he could not stand. Kathleen would puncture them all, like shards of glass under bare feet. She would never let go, she'd always be spitting questions. She would wring Stephen out again, when he had just conquered his past; just become himself.

Stephen backed his sister toward the dorm.

I'm acting as if we're hostages, he thought murkily, and Harry Donnelly has a gun. But we are, and he does. We are hostages to our history, and they have a crowbar to break in and start it up again.

"What's the matter with you?" snapped Kathleen. "Grow up, Stephen."

I am late growing up, thought Stephen, and the reason is people like you, who never left us alone.

• • •

In spite of the dry July heat, dampness covered Janie's body. She closed her eyes to keep a faint from happening and hung on to Stephen.

What will they do to me? she thought. What is happening?

Nothing can be happening! I panicked. I didn't mail it. So if I haven't mailed the letter, how does the FBI know? How could they be expecting me to contact my kidnapper? If they knew, they'd be there. They'd have Hannah in custody.

Her pulse and Stephen's raced madly and she could feel their separate fears blending and doubling, because they were not comforting each other, they were scaring each other.

What if Mr. Donnelly was here to look in her purse? What if Kathleen had told him Janie was hiding something? What were the penalties?

What am I afraid of? thought Janie. There are no penalties for me. Only for Hannah.

But that was not true. Hannah got to run barefoot in Boulder, while Janie's families suffered all the penalties.

Stephen shouted on, being a big brother, being savage. Being wrong, Janie decided finally. Harry Donnelly could only be coincidence. If he'd known about Hannah Javensen's presence, he would not have handled it as a social affair.

What is a sister? she thought dimly, hidden by Stephen's body. Should a sister protect? Shall I step aside and tell Stephen it's all right?

But whatever was happening to Stephen Spring was not all right.

She let herself be inched backward. She was Stephen's ally, and he hers, and if they had to back all the way to the East Coast, she would go with him.

• • •

Brian was gripped by fear without knowing what to be afraid of. He felt like bones inside the huge T-shirt he had borrowed from Stephen. He was cold under the shirt, which wasn't clothing anymore but a windy tent.

Johnsons: We have never been in touch with Hannah.

Springs: You must never take a risk.

What was happening here? What was the risk?

"Stephen," began Mr. Donnelly in a peaceable voice. He looked ordinary; a tall broad man in a dark suit and a red tie—he could have had any occupation.

"Get out," said Stephen. "You're not ruining this visit." His voice quivered like a failing radio signal. "My sister and my brother came to see *me*. This is a family visit. The FBI is not touching it. *Never*."

"What's the matter with you, Stephen?" snapped Kathleen. "This is my father. It's a simple visit, just like yours is a simple visit. You can be polite about it." Her sun-streaked hair fell across her face and she whipped it angrily away.

"No," said Stephen. "Having the FBI shove your sister around is never a polite kind of thing."

In Brian's memory, the FBI had not shoved. It was more that Janie had fled, half hiding under furniture, covering her eyes and whimpering, and they had followed her. That was when Brian's father ended the questions for good.

What have we done? thought Brian. We've leaped

155

feet first into more questions than any of us can face. Dear God, don't let my brother know that this is not a simple visit.

"Of course we won't talk about that," said Mr. Donnelly. "That's not dinner conversation."

"It was last time," Stephen pointed out. "I told you the situation was crummy and I didn't want to talk about it but the three of you wouldn't let it go. I don't want the FBI near my sister."

• • •

So this is what it means, thought Janie, to let the chips fall where they may.

It means, So what if your brother finds out you don't care about seeing him when you haven't seen him since Christmas? So what if he believes you missed him? So what if he finds out you're here to make everything worse?

On a graph of people she cared about, Stephen had a low rank. The people at the top were Miranda and Frank Johnson. And the chips were falling for them, too.

So what if you tried and failed, Dad? I'm doing what I want.

So what if you think the past is over, Mom? I'm doing what I want.

"Why is my father's occupation a problem, Stephen?" Kathleen asked, eyes so blue against that honey-gold complexion. "If your little kidnapette cared about you, she'd live with your family."

Kidnapette! The word mesmerized Janie. A little

girl with a little hobby—that same panicky little girl she had been at the mailbox.

Their sister, Jodie, would love that word. You are a little red-haired Barbie, Jodie would say, waving the pom-poms of your kidnapping. You kidnapette, you.

"I told you not to say that!" yelled Stephen. "Get out! Leave us alone!"

"Fine!" said Kathleen. "We're going! Have your little family reunion! See if I care!" She got back into the car and slammed the door. Her father said in a patronizing voice, "I apologize, Stephen. You should have been warned. I know you don't handle problems well. I know you aren't strong."

The car drove away, taking the curves slowly and silently, coming to a full stop at the main road, as if it might change its mind and return.

Stephen let go of his sister and fell to his knees. He doubled over, holding his stomach as if gut-shot, and retched into the grass. Nothing came up except sound.

Brian flung his thin arms around his brother. "It's okay," he said desperately. "Nothing happened. You are so strong. You do so handle problems well."

He *isn't* strong, thought Janie. He *doesn't* handle problems well.

The black Lincoln disappeared from sight and Stephen visibly breathed easier.

But Kathleen and her father were not the threat.

I'm the threat, thought Janie.

CHAPTER
SEVENTEEN

Reeve herded them all back to Stephen's room. Maybe in a small enclosed space he could think clearly, which certainly wasn't happening out here under the vast Western sky.

They shut the door after them and collapsed.

Stephen fell backward on his bed, which was unmade, sheets half out, blanket on the floor. Stephen was not the type to notice.

There were no chairs. Brian slumped against the wall, slid down until he was sitting and then flopped out flat. Reeve wadded up his sleeping bag to make a cushion for Janie and she sat on the floor.

He himself opened the window, snapped out the screen and straddled the sill, one leg hanging outside. He played with the window, maneuvering the catch, flattening his hand on the glass, twisting his wrist until he printed out a chrysanthemum of fingerprints.

Suppose Janie uncovers Hannah, he thought.

Suppose the FBI follows her or Stephen follows her or Hannah sticks to her? What happens to Stephen then? Already, his girlfriend is ruined. With Hannah discovered, school will be ruined, the year ruined, the West ruined.

And that's just Stephen.

What about everybody else? What about the Johnsons? The Springs? Janie herself?

She had written that check. Reeve had watched her do it. He did not know what else she'd done, but presumably she'd mailed it, and on Monday, it would be in Hannah's post office box, and Janie would go there, and spot Hannah, and talk to her.

He had to stop Janie from meeting Hannah. But good reasons had not stopped her and responsibility had not stopped her and calling her names had not stopped her.

He studied the whorls of his fingerprints on the glass and tried to follow little paths, little labyrinths on his own thumb. The only way to prevent Janie from meeting Hannah was to offer her a solution; an answer. Not the answer to her actual questions; she must never ask those. But some method by which Janie could get out from under Frank's stupid support decision.

But what could that solution be?

Not for the first time, Reeve wished he were as smart as his sister Lizzie. As smart as Brian, for that matter.

Finally he said, "So what's with the FBI, Stephen?" He smudged out the flower with his fist. "You acted as if Mr. Donnelly is dangerous to us."

Stephen lifted a pillow high over his head and stared up at the puffy rectangle, and then lowered it slowly, as if considering suffocating himself. "It's probably nothing. Coincidence. The kind of thing we've dealt with since the day it happened. People can't keep their hands off it. A crime happens to you, you turn into property. People touch you, and poke you; aim a camera at you; record you. You're not a person anymore, you're entertainment. Live-action crime." He cradled the pillow in his arms.

"Then . . . ," said Reeve, making new and very careful fingerprints, as if he intended them for the FBI, "the reason you were standing in front of Janie was . . . to protect her from . . ."

"Nothing, probably," said Stephen. "I guess I was being a jerk. I was lying when I said if I found the kidnapper I'd follow through and force a trial. If this started up again, I'd turn to stone."

It caught Reeve in the chest, a fist against his ribs, and he looked at Janie and said silently, Are you listening? Do you hear him?

Janie flushed and turned away from Reeve's stare. She hears him all right, thought Reeve, she's listening, but she's going to do what she wants no matter what happens afterward.

He felt sick and desperate, wanting so much for Janie to do the right thing; not wanting her to join the crowd he was in; people who didn't bother with the right thing.

"I bet Hannah Javensen wasn't planning to see her parents the day she stole you, Janie," said Stephen. "She was on the run, maybe from her own cult, we'll never know, and the kidnapping made things worse, so she threw the problem into her mother and father's living room and drove away. I bet if we ever found her and questioned her, she would hardly remember."

He flung the pillow aside. "It's as powerful as vanishing to say to a person, *So what? You're nothing to me.* And that's why I hate her and why I can't unhate. I don't think she noticed what she did to us. And that's evil."

Janie crossed her legs and tucked her toes into the corners made by her knees. She was so graceful. So worth watching, sitting like that. Reeve wanted to pack everybody in this room into the nearest rental car and start driving. Anywhere, anywhere at all, just not near Hannah and this terrible decision Janie was making.

"Stephen?" she said. She tucked her long flowery skirt over her ankles and toes and pleated the cloth in her fingers. "Sometimes I think *I* have an evil streak."

"Everybody has an evil streak," said Stephen. "You missed a lot of theology when you weren't around to go to church like the rest of us. When you feel like doing evil, you have to stomp on it." He summoned enough strength to turn his head and smile at his sister. "I stomp a lot." He hoisted himself to a sitting position, tugged at the waistband of his shorts and blew out a huge breath of air. "I lost weight dating Kathleen."

"How can you tell?" said Brian. "You've always been the diameter of a tire iron."

Stephen threw the pillow at him. It got Brian in the chest, so Brian just wrapped his arms around it. Foiled, Stephen began throwing books. Brian wasn't the twin who could catch, so he ducked and the books slammed against the wall. Stephen threw books until he'd broken the spines of every one.

He was right. He stomped a lot.

• • •

Turned to stone, thought Janie. If I had mailed my letter and met my kidnapper, I would have shoved Stephen off the cliff.

The letter, crumpled in her purse, felt as large as any Rocky Mountain.

"We all look as if we've had the flu and we've been throwing up for two days," she said. "Listen, Stephen. I know the restaurant Kathleen chose. I could take a taxi there, smooth things out, settle everything down." She thought she faked cheerfulness pretty well.

"Forget it," said Stephen.

"She's your girlfriend. You adore her."

"I was going to break up with her anyway."

"No, you weren't, Stephen. You're crazy about her."

"She thinks her questions are more important than we are," said Stephen flatly.

Oh, Kathleen! thought Janie. Me too. I totally agree. My questions are very important. How can I

162

walk away from the chance to know everything at last? I have only a few hours left. I'll never have this chance again.

"Anyway, if I had to see Kathleen or Mr. Donnelly again," said Stephen, "I'd probably have to say I'm sorry. And I'm not. I've never been sorry. I hate being sorry. I hate people who want me to say I'm sorry."

Reeve began laughing. He lost his balance and fell slowly into the room and down onto the floor, his outdoor leg scraping on the sill.

He landed at Janie's feet, still laughing, and Janie could not help herself. She put her hand on his cheek and felt the curved cheek edge of his grin. "My clothes are still in Kathleen's room," she reminded them. "I still have to spend the night there. And the night after that, too."

"You'll have a three-man escort when you go get 'em," said Brian.

"Two," said Stephen. "I'm not going."

"I can manage Kathleen," said Janie. "But if she kicks me out because she's broken up with you—"

"She doesn't know they've broken up," Brian pointed out. "She just thinks Stephen is rude. In fact, we should split before they come back with a peace offering."

Stephen catapulted off his mattress. "You think they'll come back? I can't handle that. We're out of here. Take the back stairs. Down the hall to the left. Go! Beat it!"

They flew out of the dorm, feet pounding on

stairs, doors flung open before them, on the run from Kathleen Marie.

• • •

"Okay," said Brian, frowning. "Major decision. Do I take the last slice of pepperoni and sausage or try the white cheese, fresh tomato, bacon and onion pizza? I don't like the look of white pizza. I never have."

"I'm taking the last piece of red," said Stephen, "so I guess you're going to find out what white pizza tastes like."

One skinny pale arm and one muscular tan arm shot forward. One huge grin of victory and one little-brother-beaten-again grin. The brothers dug into their pizza. Janie watched her brothers talk through mouthfuls of cheese and lose their napkins and chew the ice in their soft drinks.

My family, she thought. These people I'm just getting to know are my family. What are any answers worth when you can just go get a pizza with your own family instead?

"Let's see if we can still burp in unison," said Stephen to his brother. "Ready?"

"Me too," said Reeve. "Wait a sec. I'm not ready."

Stephen waited for Reeve and Brian to signal burp readiness and then directed a burp chorus.

The boys dissolved into garlicky laughter and something in Janie dissolved too. These two redheads were her brothers. Her actual real family. What had she thought the Springs were—room decorations?

I wanted to find Hannah Javensen so I could have power, she thought. So I could have control.

It wasn't really answers I wanted from Hannah. I wanted to shove her around, the way we were all shoved around.

But I don't want to be a person who shoves.

"Want my crusts, Janie?" said Reeve.

"You burped all over it, though."

"It's not any different from chewing all over it," he pointed out.

"Tomorrow," said Stephen, passing Janie his crusts too, "Kathleen was going to borrow a car so we could drive in the mountains. I have a bad feeling the car is her father's. So we need an alternate plan for Sunday that does not involve transportation."

Kathleen and Mr. Donnelly aren't so bad, thought Janie. They gave me a chance to see what happens when the chips fall. It isn't just Honor thy father and thy mother. It's also Honor thy big brother and thy little brother. I *have* been a kidnapette. I was going to honor myself.

Oh, Mom! she thought, and the mother in her heart was the real one; the one who had lost the terrible contest of keeping Janie. Oh, Mom, you can be proud I didn't do it in the end. I held back.

Panic hit her.

What if she *had* mailed that letter?

What if she'd dropped the crumpled old thing into the open mailbox instead of into the open purse?

She ripped the zipper open and dug frantically into her purse. Next to the crumpled envelope was her cell phone. I've never called my mother, she thought. Not once. It's been so long, Mom must be worried sick!

She whipped out the phone to call home, realizing with astonishment that it had actually been only two days.

"Oh, darling," said her mother. "How wonderful to hear your voice! I didn't want to call because I knew you'd be having such a good time. Are you having fun, darling? Are you having a splendid weekend?"

Janie had to laugh. "A splendid weekend, Mom," she agreed. "Lots and lots of fun."

Her brothers and Reeve rolled their eyes at the lies you gave to parents.

"Oh, darling, I miss you so," said her mother in Connecticut. "Daddy is still stable, so try not to worry. I feel a bit guilty because I'm terrified you'll fall in love with Colorado and I won't have you and then I'm ashamed that I want to cut your life off at the pass and stash you at home where I can lean on you."

I'm their real daughter, thought Janie.

• • •

Janie knocked lightly on the dorm room door. "Hi, Kathleen. Is it still okay for me to spend the night?"

"Of course." Kathleen gave her a bright desperate smile, her face puffy from crying.

Janie knew what it was to cry over a boy. She considered offering comfort to Kathleen but instead, after she brushed her teeth, she slid into a cotton knit

166

sleep shirt and scooted down inside the sleeping bag.

Kathleen turned out the lights. Safe in the dark, she whispered, "Is Stephen still mad at me?"

"It isn't you," said Janie, although it was. "It's our past. You treated it lightly, but it isn't light. It's dark."

Kathleen is not bad, Janie thought. She just hasn't gone through anything. She's like me two years ago, or Sarah-Charlotte and Adair and Katrina now. Great family, great life. Straight teeth, shining hair. She thinks that's what life is.

"My father really is retired from the FBI," said Kathleen. "He isn't investigating anything. He's a consultant now, he advises airports on security. That's why he was in Denver again and could drive out to Boulder. We were just curious about you. He wanted to look at you."

People loved the shiver and drama of being next to an actual kidnap victim. It was time for Janie to admit that, to shrug and answer their questions and get it over with. Put an end to melodrama.

Time, in fact, to stop being a kidnapette.

Stephen adored her, thought Janie. Maybe he still does. Maybe they will put it back together. Who am I not to help? She said to Kathleen, "Jodie would sure agree that I'm a kidnapette. After we get home, I'll tell her about it. She'll laugh for days."

She wondered if Stephen could forgive Kathleen for cramming the past back down his throat. Janie, personally, found forgiveness very hard.

When Reeve had sold her on the air just to hear the sound of his own voice—this boy who had filled her thoughts and hands and hopes—the hurt was so intense. But how minor his voice on the radio seemed now. Reeve mattered, not what he had done last year during a dumb streak.

What Reeve yelled at the races was true, she thought. If I had gone and found Hannah, I would have been betraying my parents more viciously than he betrayed me.

Reeve had become very careful around Janie, rehearsing his words, practicing his smiles, offering little gifts, like tickets to a race. It wasn't friendship when you had to be that careful.

Suddenly she couldn't stand it. All that uncertainty! All that tiptoeing!

If I were dressed, she thought, I'd race across the campus, dart up the stairs into Stephen's dorm, fling myself on top of Reeve, smashing him in his sleeping bag, flattening him on the floor, and I'd yell, Guess what! I like you again!

He'd love that.

She just might do it. She wiggled her toes to decide if she had enough energy.

In her greedy, curious voice, Kathleen said, "So what *did* Reeve do to make the Springs hate him?"

Janie slid halfway out of her sleeping bag, leaned over the floor and retrieved the huge purse. Lumpy and cold as it was, she drew it down inside the sleeping bag with her. She could imagine Kathleen rifling through it.

And as it touched her body, it touched her mind.

The nightmare was still there.

The checkbook was waiting.

Did she, or did she not, continue to support her kidnapper?

CHAPTER
EIGHTEEN

Brian was astonished and mad when, first thing Sunday morning, Kathleen and Janie knocked on Stephen's door. Hadn't they agreed that Sunday would take place without Kathleen?

Janie was giggly and hysterical and silly, the kind of girl who made Brian crazy and made him want no sisters, ever, and no girlfriends, ever, and no wife and no daughters.

Kathleen was worse. She was a fish in a tank, swimming from side to side, mouth open and fins wiggling.

Stephen just looked at them briefly and then chose a baseball cap from a long dangling rack. He jerked the cap hard down over his forehead until the bill covered his eyes.

Kathleen did all the talking. "If we don't go out in the car the way we planned, you will miss the Rockies. You cannot come out West for the first time and not go for a long mountain drive."

Kathleen won, because Stephen chose to stay silent, Janie was giggling, Brian was too little to have a vote, and Reeve couldn't figure out what team to be on.

It was the Lincoln without the father.

Kathleen got behind the wheel, beaming at Stephen and patting the front seat, but Stephen insisted Brian had to be in front and get the best window.

Great. Put *me* next to Kathleen, thought Brian.

Stephen took the middle back, drawing his knees up to his chest, and opened his geology text on his kneecaps, snapping each page, just in case Kathleen didn't notice that he didn't intend to look out any windows.

But Kathleen was right. Brian found the scenery awesome. Compared to these, Eastern mountains were tree-studded bumps. These slopes were barren and brown, but each fold of hill gave off a sense of wildlife; of cougar beyond the horizon and elk over the rim. Brian loved every mile.

Reeve, however, was not managing very well. Hour after hour, he produced long sighs, recrossing his knees, putting the window down, putting the window up, arching his back, cracking his knuckles. It became a contest between Reeve and Stephen to see who could fidget more.

"No fair," said Reeve to Stephen, "you have a book for an accessory."

Brian was jealous of the backseat. Coming home, he'd make Janie sit up here with Kathleen. He turned sadly in his seat to look at his brother.

171

"Kathleen," said Stephen, addressing her for the first time, "I think the enthusiasm for scenery is bottoming out."

Kathleen was not entirely worthless. "How's your enthusiasm for food?" she said, whipping into the parking lot of a country store.

They leaped from the car, bought sandwiches, drinks and chips and sat on benches under pines.

Brian wanted to sit next to Stephen, but Kathleen beat him to it and he had to sit next to Kathleen instead. I hate you, thought Brian, and your father is worse. Telling my brother he's not strong.

Kathleen put her arm around Brian. "I know what you're thinking."

Not likely, thought Brian.

"Whenever I'm up here," she said, "I feel as if the whole beautiful world is stretching before me. I'm in a glider, floating through the sky, and my life could land anywhere; any wonderful place at all."

• • •

Kathleen talked Stephen into walking down a trailhead with her.

The moment they were out of sight, Brian said, "Now what? What's happening, Janie? You're not going to do anything, are you? I don't want you to do anything. But Sunday will be over by the time we get back to Boulder and then we just have Monday because we fly out early Tuesday morning."

Reeve jammed garbage into a paper bag and crushed it into a smashed brown football. He tossed it in a perfect arc toward the open trash can, and in it sailed. At least I can do something right, thought Reeve. He said to Janie and Brian, "You know, Kathleen got it right. I guess even really annoying people can be right sometimes. Whatever we do here, we have to leave with the whole beautiful world before us."

Janie and Brian stared at him.

He shrugged and sipped his root beer. It came in a bottle. He liked holding a bottle to his lips much more than a can. He was exhausted from worrying about everybody. "What you have to do, Janie," he said, "is unkidnap yourself. Stephen told Brian to untwin, Stephen learned to unhate, and now you have to unkidnap."

Janie took his left hand and spread his fingers out and traced the lines on his palm. Then she turned his hand over, folding it into a fist and stroking his knuckles.

"Unkidnapping would be hard," said Brian, "because of the money. If you ignore it and skip Hannah, the money is still there. And it's bad money. You can't spend it. It's kidnap money. But if you do anything about Hannah, then what about Stephen? He said he'd turn to stone, Janie."

"I won't let him turn to stone," said Janie quietly.

Kidnap money, thought Reeve.

He felt blind and deaf, the way he did when he was close to a good idea but couldn't tap into it. He'd told Lizzie about that feeling once, and Lizzie had said, "That just means you aren't very smart, Reeve. Smart people have good ideas without having to be blind and deaf first."

173

William in love with that. What could William be like?

Brian expanded on his theory. "Every single time you're downstairs in your own house, Janie, you'll feel that money sitting there. This pile of dollars for the wrong reasons. Your questions will swarm all over you and sting you. You'll want to come back here and try again. You'll say to yourself, I can skip little problems like Stephen. Who isn't as strong as a tire iron after all, by the way."

"Nobody is," said Reeve. He moved one hand to the back of Janie's neck, a place of which he was very fond, where thick red hair met soft skin. He looked up the trailhead. No Kathleen and Stephen yet.

Reeve finished his root beer, dropped the bottle at his feet and spun it. It pointed to Janie. She looked at him. Very slowly she shifted Brian out of their way and very slowly leaned toward Reeve to place a kiss on his lips.

"Cut it out," said Brian. "We have things to decide." Brian ate his last potato chip. He looked sadly into the empty bag and said, "What that checking account really is, Janie, is a ransom. You know what I was thinking last night? In the end, Mr. Johnson paid a ransom to keep you."

Reeve's hand dropped from Janie's neck and he sat up straight, holding himself very still. *Paying a ransom.*

"We need a Trojan horse," said Brian. "We need to get into the enemy camp in such a brilliant way that Hannah doesn't realize we're there. We leave her

174

with a magnificent gift—but she opens it and it's the end of her."

• • •

Reeve began laughing. Janie remembered how much she liked the sound of his laugh. She and Brian were both caught on the laugh, and looked up at him and waited.

"Brian, you are brilliant," said Reeve. He whacked Brian on the back and then hugged him. "We've *got* a Trojan horse and we *are* going to pay a ransom."

His grin was the one Janie had loved for years, a face-splitting laugh of delight. For the first time since the radio, he looked totally proud of himself. "Janie," he said excitedly. "All that money. *It's our ransom.*"

A hundred yards away, Kathleen and Stephen were walking back. They were not touching.

"What you do, Janie," said Reeve, talking quickly, to explain everything before Kathleen and Stephen were back, "is give it all to Hannah. All at once. Now. Write a check for the entire amount. Brian's right. That's bad money. It can't be spent any way except the way Frank planned. It *is* a ransom. You *are* buying yourself back. It's your unkidnap."

Reeve had the puppy look he'd carried through high school, when all their dates were perfect.

Reeve doesn't care about Hannah, thought Janie. This is about me. He's trying to unkidnap me. Trying to pay my ransom.

He loves me.

Her eyes filled with tears again, the same childish

maddening tears, but she let go and found herself smiling, and she nodded. "It's a wonderful idea," she told him.

Her love for Reeve had evaporated, like water on the track. Now it had come back, like sweet rain.

Give all the money to Hannah. Now. In full. Not just a ransom, but an escape. A way out. Here it is, Hannah. This settles the account. You are not ours and we are not yours.

If Hannah had wanted love or parents, she would have made more than that one terrible phone call in New York. Hannah did not want love. She wanted money.

"But how will Hannah understand what we're doing?" Brian wanted to know.

He was looking at Reeve for wisdom. He too had forgiven Reeve, all the way through. Janie blinked back tears. It would be wonderful to cry, and she thought that Reeve might actually want to know that his solution was worth weeping over, but she didn't want to explain anything to Kathleen or Stephen.

"I figured that out," said Reeve. "Janie writes a note that says: This is it. You haven't done anything else well, Hannah, but this buys you a chance to do something well. It's over. Good-bye."

Not a letter to open a door, but a letter to close it, thought Janie.

Reeve's plan filled her mind, filled the crevices through which she had expected to fall and made the earth solid again. "It won't just be my ransom, Reeve," she said. "Did you realize that? I bet you

176

did. It will be my father's, too. He's the one she held hostage: his terrible knowing, when he didn't want to know. It really is a Trojan horse. We really do get into the enemy camp."

Brian was worried about loose ends. "But what if Mr. Johnson gets well, Reeve? Then what?"

"Janie writes him a letter too. If Frank gets well, he'll go to his folder in his Paid Bills and find her explanation, that we really did, once and for all, pay the bills. I bet he'll be the gladdest of all that it's over. The only good moment in a war is when the treaty is signed. He couldn't sign it," said Reeve. "You can, Janie."

She had never thought of it as war, but of course it was. The longest saddest soldier in this terrible war had been Stephen, and she had almost thrown him back in the trenches.

And Brian! Janie had actually used him to enter the battle.

I've been fighting for months, she thought. War with one family, war with another, war with Reeve, war with myself. I even flew out here to wage war with Hannah Javensen.

It's time to sign the peace treaty.

Time to unkidnap.

The fierce Western sun relaxed around her, turning soft and gold, warming her shoulders and face and heart.

I had a thousand questions. But there aren't a thousand answers. There's only one.

You do have to keep being the good guy.

CHAPTER
NINETEEN

Very early Tuesday morning, Janie and Reeve and Brian got on the airport bus. Stephen had little to say, and everybody was awkward. They hugged or shook hands and then they waved or blew kisses, but it was the kind of departure that left everybody feeling shaky and worse.

At the Denver airport, there was a delay. Reeve and Brian decided to forage for food. Janie sat at the gate with their carry-ons.

The three of them had composed the letter to Hannah, Janie had written the check and together they had mailed it. Janie had thrown the evidence of Frank's account into the trash. She'd even thrown away the disposable camera, which had never been used and yet somehow had been witness to what Janie had almost done.

She was annoyed to find herself feeling around in the big purse yet again to make sure everything she

178

needed was there and everything she didn't want to remember had been tossed out.

The purse contained something new.

A single sheet of paper folded in thirds, neither taped nor stapled.

Oh, no, thought Janie, stricken. A letter from Stephen. Did he realize why we came? Did he find out that we didn't come for him? That it wasn't a family visit?

Oh, please, no, thought Janie. Because it *was* a family visit in the end; the most family visit I've ever had.

She opened the note timidly. She did not want to find out that she was the bad guy after all.

Dear Janie,

Thanks for coming. It meant a lot. Kathleen kept saying I had to let go of you and the nightmare you represent. But she's wrong. The whole thing is about holding on.

I'm glad I bought you the boots. When you danced in the store, I felt like a million dollars.

Kathleen gave me a chance to step away from my family, and that helped. But now I have to step back to my family, and that will help even more. I think I can come home for a few weeks in August, and really visit, and really talk, and even be really glad I'm there.

*Maybe you'll come down to New Jersey
when I'm there and we'll be a real family.*

Love,
Stephen

• • •

On the plane Brian took the window, spreading his map of the United States open on his lap so that he'd know when they crossed the Missouri and the Mississippi. Janie sat in the middle and Reeve on the aisle, sprawling his long legs out into it.

"Friday night, after we get home," said Reeve to Janie, "will you go to a movie with me?"

"Friday night," said Janie, "you and I are going to Lizzie and William's wedding rehearsal." She bent down awkwardly to yank her purse out from under the seat in front of her.

"I thought Lizzie said grown-ups didn't need rehearsals," moaned Reeve. "I thought we didn't have to do that."

Janie set the purse on her lap. It was as big as a baby. She'd be glad to get rid of the thing. She unzipped the large cavity in the middle and reached inside. "William wants a rehearsal. William told your mother he will never be enough of a grown-up to go through his own wedding without practice."

Janie was a person who kept things.

Paper bracelets.

Parents.

From the depths of her purse she drew out a dusty, gritty, sticky root beer bottle. She lowered

Reeve's tray, put the bottle down on its side and gave it a spin. Reeve tried to get ready for a kiss but he was grinning too widely.

Brian was staring out the window, looking for landmarks. "Have we met William yet?" he asked.

"No," said Reeve. "What do you think he's like?"

"I bet he's perfect," said Brian. "I bet anybody Lizzie picks out would have passed every test under the sun."

Like me, thought Janie. I passed every test. Not by much. The people with the high scores would be Stephen and Brian and Reeve.

But I found my family.

I found the right thing to do.

I found the way home.

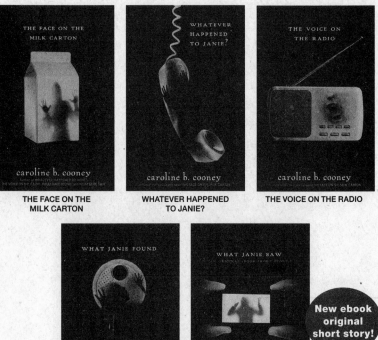

turn the page

for a sneak peek at the fifth
and final volume in the Janie series

JANIE FACE TO FACE

caroline b. cooney

Author of the bestselling novel THE FACE ON THE MILK CARTON

COMING FROM DELACORTE PRESS

THE FIRST PIECE
OF THE KIDNAPPER'S PUZZLE

The woman who had once been known as Hannah barely remembered that day in New Jersey.

It was so many years ago, and anyway, it had been an accident.

It happened because she was driving east. There was no reason to head east. But when she stole the car and wanted to get out of the area quickly, she took the first interstate ramp she saw. It was eastbound.

She had never stolen a car before. It was as much fun as drugs. The excitement was so great that she had not needed sleep or rest or even meals.

Everybody else driving on the turnpike had experience and knew what they were doing. But although the woman once known as Hannah was thirty, she had done very little driving.

Back when she was a teenager and everybody else was learning to drive, her cruel parents had never bought her a car. They rarely let her drive the family car either. They said she was immature. And in the group she joined, only the leaders had cars.

She found the group during her freshman year at college. She hated college. She hated being away from home and she hated her parents for making her go to college. Even more, she hated admitting defeat.

The group had embraced Hannah. Inside the group, she did not have to succeed or fail. There were no decisions and no worries. She did not have to choose one of those frightening things called a careers. Her parents— those people from her past—had always been on her case about her future. Always demanding that she consider her skills and abilities.

Hannah did not want to consider things.

She wanted other people to consider.

While she was still useful to the group, earning money and getting new converts, she kept the name they had given her. But time passed and the group disbanded. Its members ended up on the street. She found herself homeless and helpless, and she needed another name. For a while she called herself Tiffany. Then she tried Trixie.

In the years that followed, she made use of stolen paperwork. She was pretty good at lifting the wallets of careless college kids in coffee shops. They had too much anyway. They needed to share.

After many hours on that turnpike in that stolen car, Hannah was amazed by a sign reading WELCOME TO NEW JERSEY. She had crossed the entire country. If the road kept going, it would bump into the Atlantic Ocean. She stopped for gas. Now the signs gave directions for the Jersey Shore.

During her childhood in Connecticut, her family used to go to the beach. She didn't mind the sand, but her parents always wanted her to learn how to swim. Swimming was scary, and she refused to try, but her parents were the kind of people who forced you to do scary things. She still hated them for it. The group had told her not to worry about her mother and father. Parents were nothing; the group was her family.

No. She would not go to the beach today, because it reminded her of things better forgotten.

She got back on the interstate. It was difficult to merge with traffic. She crept along the shoulder for a while until there was finally a space. She couldn't seem to drive fast enough. People kept honking at her.

It occurred to her that she had not eaten in a long time. A billboard advertised a mall. She took the exit.

The mall was disgusting, full of American excess. People were shopping too much, eating too much, talking too much.

Her parents had been like that. They loved things. They always bought her things. They spoiled her. It was their fault that she had struggled later on.

She decided she wanted ice cream. At the food court, she was shocked by how much they charged and had to take another turn around the mall to walk off her fury. How dare they ask that much! American society was so greedy.

She took the escalator to the second floor. She was an excellent shoplifter, but she could not think of a way to shoplift ice cream. She would have to pay for it. Like the gas! She had had to pay for the gas, too!

A toddler was standing just outside a shoe shop.

Hannah did not care for small children, who were sticky and whiny. But this one was cute enough, with ringlets of red-gold hair. Hannah reached down, taking hold of those warm little fingers. The toddler gave her a beautiful smile.

The grown-ups with this child were probably only a few feet away. But they were not watching at that split second, or they would have come over. Hannah had possession. It was a hot, surging feel. A taunt-on-the-playground feel. *I have something you don't have,* sang Hannah.

She and the little girl walked to the escalator. Hannah's pulse was so fast she could have leapt off the steps and flown to the food court. Stealing a car had been much more fun than stealing a credit card. But stealing a toddler! Hannah had never felt so excited.

"What about Mommy?" said the little girl.

"She'll be here in a minute," said Hannah. And if she does come, thought Hannah, I'll say I'm rescuing the kid. I'm the savior.

Hannah giggled to herself. She was the opposite of a savior.

At the ice cream kiosk, Hannah lifted the toddler onto a stool.

"How adorable your little girl is!" cried the server. "Daddy's a redhead, huh?"

The toddler beamed.

Hannah did not.

How typical of American society that even a stupid ice cream server cared more about pretty red hair on some kid than about the suffering soul of a woman in need. The server turned to a second worker behind the counter, a skinny young man whose apron was spotted with chocolate and marshmallow. They helped each other with orders and they seemed happy.

Hannah had had a life once where people helped each other and seemed happy. But that life was gone now. The leader had been arrested, and when the group melted away, Hannah stumbled around the country, following various members, hoping they would include her in their lives again.

But they wouldn't. Grow up, they said to her. Get a life.

Hannah could not seem to get a life. It was her parents' fault. She had known that when she was a teenager. She had known that when she was in her twenties. And now she was thirty, and what did she have to show for it?

Nothing!

A stupid ice cream server had more of a life than she did!

She hated the server.

"What about Mommy?" said the little girl again. She wasn't frightened, just puzzled.

Hannah hated the cute little girl now, with her cute little outfit and her cute little barrette in her cute curly red hair. She hated the way the little girl sat so happily among strangers, assuming everybody was a friend and life was good.

You're wrong, thought the woman once known as Hannah. Nobody is a friend and life is bad.

I'll prove it to you.

CHAPTER ONE

Janie Johnson wrote her college application essay.

My legal name is Jennie Spring, but I am applying under my
other name, Janie Johnson. My high school records and SAT
scores will arrive under the name Janie Johnson. Janie Johnson is
not my real name, but it is my real life.

A few years ago, in our high school cafeteria, I glanced down at
a half-pint milk carton. The photograph of a missing child was
printed on the side. I recognized that photograph. I was the child.
But that was impossible. I had wonderful parents, whom I loved.

I did not know what to do. If I told anybody that I suspected
my parents were actually my kidnappers, my family would be
destroyed by the courts and the media. But I loved my family. I
could not hurt them. However, if I did not tell, what about that
other family, apparently my birth family, still out there worrying?

What does a good person do when there is no good thing to
do? It is a problem I have faced more than once.

I now have two sets of parents: my biological mother and
father (Donna and Jonathan Spring) and my other mother and
father (Miranda and Frank Johnson). The media refers to the
Johnsons as "the kidnap parents." But the Johnsons did not
kidnap me, and they did not know there had been a kidnapping.

Usually when people find out about my situation, they go

online for details. I have friends who have kept scrapbooks about my life. Among the many reasons I hope to be accepted at your college is that I ache to escape the aftermath of my own kidnapping. It happened fifteen years ago, so it ought to be ancient history. But it isn't. People do not leave it or me alone. It is not that distant crime they keep alive. It is my agony as I try to be loyal. "Honor thy father and mother" is a Bible commandment I have tried to live by. But if I honor one mother and father, I dishonor the other.

If I am accepted at a college in New York City, I can easily visit both sets of parents—taking a train out of Penn Station to visit my Spring family in New Jersey or a train out of Grand Central to visit my Johnson family in Connecticut. I need my families, but I don't want to live at home, because then I would have to choose one over the other.

New York City is full of strangers. I don't want to be afraid of strangers anymore. I want to be surrounded by strangers and enjoy them. It is tempting to go to school in Massachusetts, because I have relatives and a boyfriend there. But I would lean on them, and I want to stand alone. I've never done that. It sounds scary. But it is time to try.

I know my grades are not high enough. My situation meant that I went back and forth between two high schools. At my high school in Connecticut, where I grew up, and knew everybody, people were riveted by what was happening to me. They were kind, but they wanted to be part of it, as if I were a celebrity instead of somebody in a terrible position trying to find the way out. At my high school in New Jersey, my classmates had all grown up with my New Jersey brothers and sister, and they knew about the crime in a very different way, and sometimes acted as if I meant to damage my real family. As a result, I didn't study hard enough. I promise that I will study hard enough at college.

I am asking you to accept me as a freshman, but I have something even more important to ask. Whether you accept me or not, will you please not talk about me with your faculty, your student body, or your city? Thank you.

She was accepted.

The Spring parents (the real ones) and the Johnson parents (the other ones) argued with Janie about her decision to attend college in Manhattan. "It's too much for you," they said. "You can't deal with the pressure. You'll drop out. You need to be with people who know your whole history."

No, thought Janie Johnson. I need to be with people who do not know one single thing.

The New York City dormitory to which she had been assigned held six hundred kids. She would be nobody. It was a lovely thought. She did worry that she might introduce herself ("Hi. My name is Janie Johnson") and they would say, "Oh, you're the one who went and found your birth family and then refused to live with them. You're the one the court had to order to go home again. You're the one who abandoned your birth family a second time and went back and lived with your kidnap parents after all."

Outsiders made it sound easy. As if she could have said to the only mother and father she had ever known, "Hey—it's been fun. Whatever. I'm out of here," and then trotted away. As if she could have become a person named Jennie Spring over a weekend.

One reason the kidnap story was so often in the news was that Janie was photogenic. She had masses of bright auburn curls, and a smile that made people love her when she hadn't said a word.

For college, she wanted to look different.

Her sister, Jodie (the one Janie hadn't met until they were both teenagers), had identical hair, but Jodie trimmed hers into tight low curls. Janie had enough problems with this sister; imitating her hairstyle did not seem wise. So for college, Janie yanked her hair back, catching it in a thick round bun because it was too curly to fall into a ponytail.

Back when she'd first arrived at her birth family's house, Janie had shared a bedroom with the new sister, Jodie, and a bathroom with all the rest of the Springs. There were so many of them—a new mother, a new father, a big brother Stephen, an older sister Jodie, and younger twin brothers Brian and Brendan. If there was a way to say or do the wrong things with any of these people, Janie found it.

Now, when she looked back—which wasn't far; it had happened only three years ago—she saw a long string of goofs and stubbornness. If only I had been nicer! she sometimes said to herself.

But being nice in a kidnap situation is tough.

Janie's college essay spilled more truth than she had ever given anybody but her former boyfriend, Reeve. Still, it omitted two other reasons for going to college.

She wanted to make lifelong girlfriends. Sarah-Charlotte would always be her best friend, but on some disturbing level, Janie wanted to be free of Sarah-Charlotte; free to go her own way, whatever that was, and at her own speed, whatever that was.

And she wanted to meet the man who would become her husband.

Janie still loved Reeve, of course. But the boy next door had hurt her more than anyone. Whenever he was home from college (he was three years ahead of her), Reeve would plead, "I was stupid, Janie. But I'm older and wiser."

He was older, anyway. And still the cutest guy on earth. But wiser? Janie didn't think so.

Reeve was a boyfriend now only by habit. She and Reeve texted all the time, and she followed his Facebook page. She herself didn't have a photograph or a single line of information on her own wall; she was on Facebook solely to see what other people were doing. She never posted.

Janie's other mother, Miranda Johnson, was excited and worried for Janie. Miranda's life had collapsed, and this year, she was living through Janie. Miranda was so eager to see Janie launched at the university. It was Miranda who drove Janie into the city on the day her college dorm opened.

Later, Janie learned that each of her Spring parents had arranged to take that day off from work so that *they* could bring her to college. But Janie said no to them, which she had pretty much said ever since they first spoke on the phone. ("Is it the only syllable you know?" her brother Stephen once demanded.)

On the first day of college, Janie and her mother took the dorm elevator to the fifth floor and found her room. The single window had a sliver view of the Hudson River. Janie could hardly wait for her mother to leave so she could begin her new life. She refused Miranda's help unpacking and nudged her mother back into the hall, where Miranda burst into tears. "Oh, Janie, Janie! I'll miss you so, Janie!"

Janie tried to stand firm against her mother's grief. If she herself broke down, she might give up and go home.

The hall was packed with everybody else moving in, each freshman glaring silent warnings to their own parents: *Don't even think about crying like that woman.*

"Good-bye, Janie!" cried her mother, inching backward. "I love you, Janie!"

At last the elevator doors closed and Janie was without a parent. She sagged against the wall. Had she done the right thing? Should she run after Miranda and somehow make this easier?

A friendly hand tapped her shoulder. "Hi. I'm Rachel. And you are definitely Janie!"

Everyone in the hall was smiling gently. In minutes, she knew Constance and Mikayla and Robin and Samantha. Nobody bothered with last names. I can skip my last names! thought Janie.

"I'm actually Jane," she said. "Only my mother calls me Janie." She had never been called Jane. She felt new and different and safe, hiding under the new syllable along with the new hair. "Jane" sounded sturdier than "Janie." More adult.

Her actual roommate appeared so late that Janie had been thinking she might not even have a roommate. "Eve," said the girl, who flung open the door around eleven o'clock that night. "Eve Eggs. I've heard every joke there is. Do not use my last name. You and I will be on a first-name basis only."

"I'm with you," said Janie.

Her new friends—girls who seemed so poised, and whose grades and SAT scores were so much higher than Janie's—were nervous in the Big Apple. They thought Janie was the sophisticated one. Everybody she knew back home would think that was a riot.

Rachel loved ballet and wanted Janie to help her find Lincoln Center.

Constance wanted Janie to teach her how to use the subway.

Mikayla had planned to study fashion, but her parents said fashion was shallow and stupid, so Mikayla ended up here, and wanted Janie to take her to fabulous New York stores and fashion districts that dictated what women would wear.

Eve had a list of famous New York places, and wanted to see them with Janie.

Janie did it all. She even managed to alternate weekend visits with the Springs in New Jersey and the Johnsons in Connecticut. Every

Sunday morning, she'd catch an early train and go for brunch with one family or the other.

When she met her academic advisor, the man did not seem to know her background. In fact, he kept glancing at his watch, resentful that thirty minutes of his precious time was being spent on her. She loved it. Maybe the sick celebrity of being a kidnap victim was over.

When her sister, Jodie, came into the city for a weekend visit, Janie primed her. "They know nothing. They don't even know my last name! I'm just a girl named Jane. It's so great. Like having my own invisibility cloak."

Jodie was always prickly. "You enrolled here as a Johnson," she snapped. "Which happens to be your kidnap name. If you really don't want to be a kidnap victim, you would use your real name. You'd be Jennie Spring."

It's true, thought Janie. *I'm* the one extending the situation. I shouldn't have changed my name from Janie to Jane. I should have changed my name to Jennie Spring.

And if she said that out loud, Jodie would point out that being Jennie Spring was not a name change. It was her name.

When their weekend came to a close, Jodie said, "I have to admit that I thought being away from your Connecticut home would destroy you. But you're doing fine. You're Miss Personality here."

"I had plenty of personality before," said Janie.

"Yes, but it was annoying."

They giggled crazily, and suddenly Janie could hug Jodie the way she'd never been able to. "I was annoying," she admitted. "I was worthless and rude."

"Totally," said Jodie. "But now you're fun and rational. Who could have predicted that?"

Janie laughed. "I'm coming home for the summer," she told her sister.

"Home?" Jodie was incredulous. "You mean, my house? That home?"

"If you want me."

"Oh, Janie, we've always wanted you. *You* never wanted *us*!"

The wonderful weeks of freshman year flew by.

Eve began talking about Thanksgiving. Eve's family had several hundred traditions, including who mashed the potatoes and who chopped the celery for the turkey stuffing. "I have the most wonderful new family here," Eve said, "especially you, Jane, but I can hardly wait to get home to my real family."

Even Eve, with whom Janie shared every inch of space and many hours a day and night, did not know that Janie Johnson had both a real family and another family. Like everybody else in the dorm, Eve vaguely assumed there had been a divorce and remarriage.

In contrast, Mikayla and Rachel acted as if they barely remembered home, family, and Thanksgiving. Janie could now see why parents might dread the departure for college: that beloved child could put away the last eighteen years like a sock in a drawer.

For Janie, the last eighteen years was more like clothing she had never been able to take off, never mind forget.

Janie telephoned her real mother. "Mom?" she said to Donna. It had taken her three years to use that word with Donna and just as much time to think of the Springs' house as home. "May I come home for Thanksgiving?"

"Yes!" cried her real mother. "Everybody's going to be here. Stephen's coming from Colorado and Jodie's coming from Boston! Brian promised not to study on Thanksgiving Day, and Brendan promised not to have a ball game."

The twins were still in high school. Brian was still academic and Brendan was still athletic. Brian was always part of the Sunday brunch when Janie came out to New Jersey, but Brendan never was. If he didn't have a game, he went to somebody else's.

Next Janie planned the difficult call to her other mother.

A few years ago, her other father had had a serious stroke. Miranda was not strong enough to move and lift Frank. Over the summer, while Janie was preparing to move herself to a college dorm, she had also moved her parents into an assisted living institution, where Frank was much better off. For poor Miranda, it was prison. Miranda should have found herself her own apartment close to all her girlfriends and volunteer work and ladies' lunches and golf. But she could not bear to live alone or to abandon Frank to loneliness.

Miranda would be counting on Janie's presence for Thanksgiving.

Miranda did not know how to text and rarely emailed. She loved to hear Janie's voice, so in this call, as in others, Janie started with gossip about Eve, Rachel, and Mikayla. Finally she came to the hard part. "For Thanksgiving, Mom?" Her throat tightened and her chest hurt. She hadn't even said it yet and she was swamped by guilt. "I'm going to take the train to New Jersey on Wednesday and spend Thanksgiving Day and Friday with them."

"New Jersey" was code for Janie's birth family; "them" meant the Springs.

"Saturday morning I'll get myself to Connecticut and stay until Sunday afternoon with you," she added brightly. "Then you'll drive me to the train station Sunday night so I can get back to the city."

Miranda's voice trembled. "What a good idea, darling. If you came here, we'd have to eat in the dining room with a hundred other families and the cranberry sauce would come out of a can."

Normally, Janie caved when her mother's voice trembled. But Jodie's visit had been profound. The name change, and the soul change, could not be from Janie to Jane. It had to be from Janie to Jennie. All the vestiges of the kidnap, even the ones she cherished, needed to end. She wasn't ready yet. But in her mental calendar of life, becoming Jennie Spring was not too many months away.

"I know it won't be the perfect Thanksgiving for you, Mom," Janie said, which was a ridiculous remark. It would be awful for Miranda. "But I'll see you on Saturday, and that will be great. I love you."

"Oh, honey. I love you too."

Vacation by vacation, Janie slid out of the Johnson family and into the Spring family. The Springs rejoiced; the Johnsons suffered.

When freshman year ended, Janie divided her summer. She lived Monday through Friday with her birth family. She got a job at a fish fry restaurant. She came home with her hair smelling of onions and grease. Fridays she worked through lunch, went home, shampooed the stink out of her hair, and caught the train from New Jersey into New York. From there, she took a subway to Grand Central, and another train out to Connecticut, where her mother picked her up at the station. Her father always knew her. Frank could smile with the half of his mouth that still turned up, and sometimes make a contribution to the conversation. But mostly, he just sat in his wheelchair.

A few years ago, when Frank suffered the first stroke, Miranda stayed at the hospital while Janie handled the household. Janie was struggling with bills when she stumbled on a file in Frank's office. To her horror, she found that Frank had always known where his daughter Hannah was and had sent her money every month. Of course, for twelve of those years, neither he nor anybody else dreamed that Hannah had kidnapped Janie. But when the face on the milk carton was produced and the truth came out, when the FBI and the police and the media and the court got involved, Frank Johnson knew exactly where the criminal was, and he never breathed a word. He had been writing a check to

Janie's kidnapper on the very day the FBI was interrogating him.

It had been such a shock to learn that she was a kidnap victim. But Janie almost buckled when she understood that her father was aiding and abetting the kidnapper. Only to Reeve did Janie spill the secret. One of the comforts of Reeve was that he knew everything. It was always a relief to be with the one person who knew it all.

And then came another surprise: at college, she found out that it was more peaceful to be among people who knew nothing.

During freshman year, Janie saw Reeve only at Thanksgiving and Christmas. The summer after freshman year, Janie saw him only once, at the fabulous college graduation party his parents gave him. It was so much fun. Reeve had more friends than anybody, and they all came, and it was a high school reunion for his class. He and Janie were hardly alone for a minute. During that minute, he curled one of her red locks around a finger, begging her to come back to him.

She didn't trust herself to speak. She shook her head and kissed his cheek.

He didn't know why she couldn't forgive him. She didn't know either.

The following day, Reeve left for good. He had landed a dream job in the South and had to say good-bye to her in front of people. His departure was stilted and formal. She said things like "Good luck" and he said things like "Take care of yourself." And then it was over: the boy next door had become a man with a career.

Her heart broke. But she wanted a man she could trust, and she only half trusted Reeve. It was so painful to imagine him lost to her, living a thousand miles away and leading a life about which she knew nothing. She kept herself as busy as she could. One good thing about her parents' move to the Harbor was that they no longer lived next door to Reeve's family: she no longer used the driveway on which she and Reeve learned to back up; no longer saw the yard on which they raked leaves; no longer ran into Reeve's mother and got the updates she both yearned for and was hurt by, because she wasn't part of them.

By July that summer, Janie was not visiting her Connecticut parents until Saturday mornings. By August, she was borrowing her real mother's car, driving up for lunch on Saturdays, and driving home to New Jersey the same night. As her visits dwindled, so did her Connecticut mother. Miranda became frail and gray.

Is it my fault? thought Janie. Or is it just life? Am I responsible for keeping my other mother happy? Or is Miranda responsible for starting up new friendships and figuring out how to be happy again? I'm eighteen. Do I get to have my own life on my own terms? Or do I compromise because my mother is struggling?

The only person with whom she could share this confusion was Reeve. But she had decided not to share.